Jacob Piatt Dunn

History of Indiana

Jacob Piatt Dunn

History of Indiana

ISBN/EAN: 9783742825186

Manufactured in Europe, USA, Canada, Australia, Japa

Cover: Foto ©Andreas Hilbeck / pixelio.de

Manufactured and distributed by brebook publishing software
(www.brebook.com)

Jacob Piatt Dunn

History of Indiana

HISTORY OF INDIANA.

J. P. DUNN.

T was in the year 1800 that the name "Indiana" was first applied to the region now included in the state. For thirty years or more before that time, when Indiana was mentioned in this country, the reference was to a tract of land lying in what is now West Virginia, and forming in part the county of Indiana in that state. This tract was a famous Indian land grant, which was the subject of much discussion in the old continental congress, and a bone of contention in the politics of those days, though now it is chiefly of interest as having suggested the name for this state. In 1800 it was Indiana territory, of course, and that year forms a convenient dividing line between the great epochs of the past and the present of the state. At that time Indiana was still a wilderness, chiefly the home of wild beasts and wild men. In the vast extent of the territory, which included practically all of what is now the states of Indiana, Illinois, Michigan, Wisconsin and Minnesota, there were less than 6,000 white people, and less than half of them lived in what is now Indiana. There were about 1,500 in and about the town of Vincennes, on the Wabash, the capital city of the new territory; a few scattered along the Wabash at Indian villages; nearly a thousand in Clark's Grant, on the Ohio, and two or three hundred on the lower Whitewater, in the southeastern corner of the state, which was temporarily included in Ohio. The Indian title had not been extinguished in any part of our present territory except these three places, and a few small locations for military posts. The southern and central portions of the state

—from the Ohio to the Wabash—were covered with a heavy forest, with but a few small prairies in the northern and western parts.

It is evident that the Indiana of to-day is a development since that date. Before 1800 lies a long period of interesting and romantic history, but it is not the history of the development of a people into a great commonwealth. It is the record of the progress of hardy explorers into an unknown land, of the transactions of traders with the natives, of the establishment of military posts to maintain the claims of European kings, of wars that were the echoes of quarrels across the ocean and were of more importance here in their ultimate results than in bloodshed. When more than a century of all this had passed, and the year 1800 was reached, Indiana was still a wilderness, with only three little spots where the whites had secured a foothold within her borders, and these barely within her borders. Think what a change has been wrought since then! Think of the gigantic physical task of clearing away the trackless forests and bringing the land under cultivation, of opening roads, of building towns and cities, of banding the state with lines of railroad and telegraph. Men sometimes speak with wonder of the work accomplished by the persistent effort of the coral insect, but here is an accomplishment quite as wonderful. Did you ever watch a woodman cut down a tree? Have you noted how slow the process, chip by chip, chip by chip, until the trunk is eaten through? Consider, then, the application of this process to forests covering over half the state of Indiana. And this was but preliminary work, for after it was done, and the trunks disposed of, and the underbrush grubbed out, there was but preparation for the planting of crops to sustain life and to produce the wealth for the future advance of the state.

And this result of physical effort alone was not the most wonderful, for with it has come an industrial development that has utilized every advantage that nature offered. Not only has the face of the earth been made to yield its increase, but the hoarded treasures of its depths have been opened and brought into use. For the conversion of these products into all the uses that the wit of man has devised, the arts and sciences have been called into action in Indiana, and her manufactures are now shipped into every part of the earth. And above all, this progress in material things has been the development of a social organization that compares without disadvantage with that of the oldest and proudest of civilized nations. It is a state of intelligent and happy homes. It is a state of well-governed cities and towns. It is a state whose laws have served as models for older states. Its system of charities and corrections has received wide commendation. Its educational system has attracted the attention and admiration of students of educational science. Indiana is not laggard. It stands in the front ranks, and is pushing forward and upward without ceasing. And what does all this mean? These things are not the result of climate, or soil, or location, or natural products. They are the work of men. The true history of Indiana is in the lives of her people, the men of progress who have laid hold of this rough jewel and shaped and polished it until it is a gem of purest ray. The record of the advance of the state through the various stages is but the meager outline of the lives of the men who caused those advances by their united, patient and admirable efforts. Their good works can never be fully written, but the following pages present some samples from which the rest may be in part imagined, and preliminary to these personal portrayals it is desirable to sketch the outlines of the history of the state to whose greatness they have contributed.

THE ABORIGINAL INHABITANTS.

As in the other states, the earliest traces of human life in Indiana are the remains of that mysterious race, the mound builders. Who they were nobody knows, but it is reasonably assured that they had no connection with any inhabitants of the state of whom we have knowledge. They must have lived here long before the Indian tribes, and their bones, their architecture, their arts and their numbers all prove that they were of a different race. It is certain that they were quite numerous in this region, and it is possible that a large part of the state was under cultivation in their day, for the forests grew as heavy over their mounds and earthworks when the white men first knew them as on any of the other land. Many of their works are found in the state, especially in the southern counties. Some of the defensive works are large, covering an area of over thirty acres and others are built with remarkable military skill. They have furnished ample material for the study and speculation of the learned and curious, but they remain unsolved problems as they were at first. Beyond this field of conjecture the mounds and the men who made them have had nothing to do with the known history of Indiana.

The earliest Indian claim to this territory that is known was made by the Miamis, and it was conceded by the other tribes, but it is not at all certain that they had resided within the borders of the state long before the French explorers came. They claimed all the land north of the Ohio river from the Wabash to the Scioto and extending north to a line drawn from Chicago to Detroit. Within these limits their ownership was not seriously questioned by other Indians, but they were very hospitable in granting territory to their allies, and the tribal relations became so broken that there is much confusion concerning them. Mr. Gallatin, who aimed to classify the Indians according to language, put the Miamis under the head of the "Western Lenape," with the Menominees, the Illinois, the Sacs and Foxes, the Kickapoos and Mascoutins, and the Piankeshaws. All these nations belong to the Algonquin family, and are evidently descended from a common stock. In the earliest period of exploration of our territory the Miamis, in part at least, were living in the northen part of the state, above the Wabash, and the southern part of the state was uninhabited. In the year 1682-3, LaSalle induced all of the Miamis, and all the other Indians that afterward lived in Indiana, to join his colony on the Illinois river. After his death the colony went to pieces and our tribes slowly made their way to the east, most of them having centered about Detroit by the year 1712. The movement to the south, and the establishment of the tribes on the Wabash, as they subsequently were known to the whites, occurred soon after this time.

The Pottawatomies resided chiefly in the lower peninsula of Michigan, but also made claim to Indiana as far south as the Wabash. This land was also claimed by the Miamis, but the two tribes occupied it jointly. Although they took part in the principal wars the Pottawatomies were rather quiet in disposition and most of them professed adherence to Catholocism. They were very much opposed to removal from the state, and were in fact taken away by force, but they have done very well in their western homes—much better than the other Indians from this state.

The tribal organization of the Miamis is not very definitely understood. De Vaudreuil in 1718 divided them simply into Miamis and Ouiatenons, the latter including all who lived on the Wabash. Chauvignerie, in 1736, says they are divided into two principal families,"the crane and the elk, though some have the bear." Those of the crane totem appear to have kept pretty well together, as the band living on the Maumee were commonly called Twightwees (from the cry of the crane twah-twah), and the other Miamis called them "the older brothers." De Vaudreuil estimated the Miamis at 400 warriors, and the Ouiatenons, including the Piankeshaws, Pepikokias, Eel Rivers and La Gros, at about 1,000 to 1,200 warriors. Col. Bouquet, in 1764, divided our Indians into Miamis 400,

Kickapoos 300, Ouiatenons 400, and Piankeshaws 250. At the beginning of the revolutionary war the tribes were estimated at Miamis 300, and Piankeshaws, Musketoons (Mascoutins) and Vermillions 800. All these estimates are on the basis of one warrior to five persons. Mr. Gallatin divided the Miamis into the Miamis proper or Twightwees, the Eel Rivers and the Ouiatenons. The second division included the band occupying the village at the mouth of Eel river, called Kenapacomaqua—the present site of Logansport. They were sometimes known by the French name L'Anguille, or as Volney's translator corrupts it, "Long Isles." The Ouiatenons, whose name is found in all sorts of fanciful variations, from "Wawyachtenokes" or "Wayoughtanies" to "Ouijas," or "Weas," were located just below the site of Lafayette. Associated with these were the remnants of the Kickapoos and Mascoutins, who had also been a part of LaSalle's confederacy, but who were almost exterminated in war with the French and the other Indians in 1712. Lower down on the Wabash were the Piankeshaws, also members of LaSalle's confederacy, and now closely allied with the Miamis. The Delawares came into Indiana about the middle of the last century, and were granted lands for residence by the Miamis on White river. The Shawnees, of whom there were never many in Indiana, came at a still later date. It is not probable that there were ever 10,000 Indians residing within the borders of Indiana at any time after it was visited by the whites, but they were allied with all the other Indians of the northwest in their warfare against the Americans, and jointly they were able to do a great deal of damage.

During the French occupancy the Indians gave very little trouble until the English began their movement into the Ohio valley and won a part of the Indians to their support. From that time there were hostilities of more or less importance, but most of the Indians sided with the French to the close of the French and Indian war. When the French abandoned the contest, the Indians continued their opposition to the British, and under the brilliant leadership of Pontiac managed to keep the British out of the northwest for two years longer. Then they made peace with the British, and remained their faithful allies to the close of the revolutionary war. After the close of that war they resisted the entrance of the Americans north of the Ohio, and were encouraged and abetted by the British, who wished to keep an independent Indian state as a "buffer" between the Americans and the English possessions. This was the period of most of the Indian troubles in Indiana, and it was ended by Wayne's victory in 1795, and the treaty of Greenville in the same year, by which the Indian title to the small tracts of land mentioned as occupied by the whites in 1800 was extinguished.

The tide of immigration made it desirable to open more land to settlement, and vigorous efforts to do this were begun. The southern part of the state was entirely uninhabited, and treaties were made in 1804 and 1805 by which the lands along the Ohio running back for thirty or forty miles were acquired from the Piankeshaws and Delawares. These cessions did not arouse much opposition from the Indians, but a little later Tecumseh and his brother the Prophet returned to Indiana and began the formation of a confederacy of the northwestern tribes to protect their hunting grounds from further encroachments by the whites. The times were propitious, for continued friction of daily life had aroused the feeling of hostility between whites and Indians. In 1809 treaties were made for the purchase of two tracts of land, one running some thirty miles north of the Vincennes tract, and bounded by what was known as "the ten o'clock line," and the other running twelve miles west from the Greenville treaty line. Only a part of the Indians joined in these treaties, and Tecumseh earnestly opposed them. The attitude of the Indians grew more hostile until in 1811 Gov. Harrison took the field against them and defeated them at the battle of Tippecanoe. The troops under Harrison numbered about 1,000 and the Indians have been variously estimated at from 350 to 730, with probabilities nearer the larger number.

After this fight there was comparative quiet until the war of 1812 began, and then most of the Indians went to the aid of the British. During that war the most important Indian warfare in Indiana occurred—Pigeon Roost massacre, the attack on Fort Harrison, the siege of Fort Wayne, the battle of Mississinewa and numerous smaller massacres and encounters. In 1815 the Indians ceded practically all the land south of the Wabash except a few reserves, and by supplemental treaties in 1818 surrendered additional lands above the Wabash. There were no real Indian hostilities in the state after 1815, but only a few acts of individual lawlessness. In 1826 and 1828 the Miamis and Pottawatomies relinquished their general claims and took reservations. From 1834 to 1838 they surrendered their reservations and were removed west of the Mississippi except a few individuals who retained lands in Indiana that have been assigned in severalty. It was but a wretched remnant that was removed—less than 400 Weas and Piankeshaws and 1,100 Miamis—but it went to pieces still more rapidly in the new prairie home. Dissipation and disease did deadly work, and during the civil war and the Kansas troubles preceding it they seemed exposed to every untoward influence. Under the leadership of Baptiste Peoria, part of the Miamis and Weas reformed and made some progress, but when the remnants of the tribes were gathered up and moved to Quapaw reservation in 1873 there were only about 150 left. Probably a part had scattered and mixed with other Indians or with whites, but most of them had disappeared forever.

There is no room for question that the worst enemy of the Indians of Indiana was whiskey. The records by observers of their awful debauches are too numerous and too uniform to leave any doubt. So long as they remained in this state there was no prohibition of liquor on the reservations, and it was sold in unlimited quantities by the licensed traders at the distributions of annuities. The Indians went into their drunks systematically and unanimously. Everybody in the tribe got drunk and stayed drunk as long as liquor could be procured. Their fatal passion for drink meant to them destitution, disease and death. The reduction of their numbers by 75 per cent. from the beginning of the revolutionary war to 1836 was due chiefly to this cause, as was most of their decrease after their removal from the state. At the beginning of the revolutionary war the Indians of the Wabash were approaching a semi-civilized state. They cultivated corn quite extensively, and raised some potatoes, cabbage and turnips. They had some fruit trees, bred some poultry and pigs and had a few cattle. They compared very favorably with the Creeks and Choctaws at that time. But in their war with the Americans, for the first time in a century, they were struck in their homes. Expedition after expedition swooped down on them from the great forest as noiselessly and as mercilessly as they ever fell upon a frontier cabin. Their villages were burned, their stores of corn destroyed, their fields ravished. In the vicissitudes of that long struggle they lost much of the advance they had made, and in the succeeding years they did no more than to regain their lost ground, if so much.

It is not commonly known that at the time of the discovery of America the Indians generally were cannibals, but such is the fact, and many of them continued in this practice for at least two centuries later. The early chronicles recount numerous instances of it, and the evidences of its prevalence are beyond question. With the Miamis it continued longer than with other tribes, but with them it became a sort of religious ceremony, and was restricted to a society or brotherhood, such as is commonly formed among Indians for various purposes. The latest recorded instance of the practice was near the close of the revolutionary war, when a young Kentuckian was killed and eaten at the site of Ft. Wayne. The immediate cause of the decadence of cannibalism was the growth of slavery. Both the British and the

French colonists were slaveholders, and from motives of humanity ransomed prisoners from the Indians to save them from torture and death. Of course if the released captive was a negro or an Indian he was held in slavery. The Indians soon found that their prisoners had an exchange value in goods and firewater superior to their taste for human flesh, and so cannibalism died out and slavery arose. Frequently the wealthier Indians held slaves themselves. Among the Algonquin tribes an Indian slave was called a "pani," as the French wrote it, which is .equivalent to our English "Pawnee." The name undoubtedly came originally from personal reference to Indian slaves of that nation. The panis formed a considerable part of the slave population among the French settlers of Indiana and negroes captured by the Indians from the British settlements formed another considerable part.

THE FOREIGN DOMINION.

The first white men who trod the soil of Indiana were French, and by virtue of discovery and settlement France held the region until it was wrested from her by England in war. The first explorer to come was Robert Cavalier, Sieur de la Salle, who explored the Ohio river along the southern boundary of the state in 1669-70, and passed through the northwestern part of the state—up the St. Joseph's, across the South Bend portage, and down the Kankakee—in 1671-72. This was merely exploration in the interest of his fur trading business, the headquarters for which was at Fort Frontenac, on Lake Ontario. Ten years later he undertook to establish a great trading center on the Illinois, in the midst of the great concession which the French king had given him. The Iroquois came across the country from their New York homes and destroyed this establishment once, but he restored it, and gathered about it all the Indians of the northwest, including those of Indiana, as has been mentioned. The Iroquois came no more, but the trend of travel and settlement was turned from the Wabash country for the time being. A remarkable confusion has grown up in the early history of Indiana at this period from the fact that the French, following the Indian custom, treated the Wabash and the lower Ohio as one stream, and continued the name "Ouabache" to the Mississippi river. In the year 1702 a post was built at the mouth of the Ohio river, where Cairo now stands, and as it was spoken of in old chronicles as being "on the Ouabache," our earlier writers supposed it to be Vincennes. So far as is known there were neither whites nor Indians on the Wabash at that time.

As has been said, the Indians began coming back early in the eighteenth century and there were French traders with them in their larger settlements. This return movement was encouraged by the French on the theory of protecting the country from encroachments of the English, but hardly were the Indians re-established than the French became fearful that their savage allies would be won over to the British, whose traders were very enterprising and aggressive. An effort was then made to induce the Indians to retire from the Wabash again, but without success. Failing in this the French adopted the policy of establishing small military posts among them, and putting in command Frenchmen who had strong personal influence with them. The first of these establishments was made at the site of Fort Wayne, some time earlier than 1718, and the second was Post Ouiatenon, on the north side of the Wabash, just below Lafayette, which was established a year or two later. These were not settlements but only trading posts, and were not of a permanent character, though the fur trade at them was large and important. Post Vincennes was established about the year 1727 and in 1735 a number of families settled there. It was the first permanent French settlement in Indiana, and the only one of the general character of a white settlement, where agriculture was an industry of importance. There was another post on the St. Joseph's river, but it was beyond our borders, near the site of Niles, Michigan.

These posts were merely small parts of a great colonial system. Vincennes was included in the province of Louisiana and the district of Illinois. It had a commandant whose immediate superior resided at Ft. Chartres, on the Mississippi, and his superior was located at New Orleans. The other posts were in the province of Canada, and were governed from Detroit. The government was very simple, being of a military character, with practically all the power in the commandant. The founder of Post Vincennes, and first commandant, was Francois Margane, Sieur de Vincennes. In 1736, with the other forces from the Illinois, he marched against the Chickasaw Indians, in what is now Mississippi, and was there killed in battle. His successor was Louis Groston, commonly known as St. Ange, who commanded until the country was surrendered to the English. The commandant exercised the power of granting concessions of land to individuals, and his acts were certified by the notary, who was the only other functionary of importance at the post.

The French settlers at Vincennes had a common field of about 5,400 acres, which was fenced in, and in which the cattle belonging to the village were kept. The individual concessions were outside, and were not fenced. The concessions were laid off in long narrow strips, so that the homes of the owners might be thrown near each other. They were a very sociable and neighborly people. Their agriculture was rude, but the soil was fertile. They raised large amounts of wheat and corn, as well as vegetables and some fruits. They made wine of the wild grapes, and sugar from maple sap. They raised tobacco of very good quality, and devoted considerable attention to the cultivation of indigo. They had cattle and hogs in abundance, and some horses. They cultivated hops, and brewed beer in small quantities. They made linen from the wild hemp. In religion they were, of course, all Catholics. The Wabash country was first laid off as a missionary district in 1726, and a missionary priest was sent over from France to take charge of it, but the record of his work has disappeared. The oldest church records date back only to 1749. The manners and customs of these early settlers were the same as those of the inhabitants of Canada and Louisiana, with whom they were one people, but the influx of Americans in our region was so rapid, and so large in proportion to the existing colonization, that very few traces of the old French civilization are to be found except at Vincennes and in a less degree at Ft. Wayne.

The change to British rule had very little effect on the Indiana posts except to deprive them of the regular control which had existed before. From the departure of St. Ange in May, 1764, the government was very uncertain. Pontiac and his Indians kept the British out of the country for two years after the war had closed, and even then no one came to take possession of the Indiana posts for a long time. In 1772, Gen. Gage, who commanded over that region, peremptorily ordered all the whites out of the Indian country, and it was only after petition and proof that their homes had been regularly granted to them that they were permitted to remain. Finally, in 1777, Lieut.-Gov. Abbott came down from Detroit and devoted nearly a year to adjustment of the affairs of the region. But in January, 1778, he was recalled, and the posts were left to take care of themselves. At this time George Rogers Clark made his celebrated expedition against the Illinois settlements, which he captured and reconciled to American rule more by diplomacy and intimidation than by force of arms. When he proposed to march against Post Vincennes two of the Frenchmen at Kaskaskia, Dr. Lafonte and Father Gibault, volunteered to go there and win the people over to the American cause. The offer was accepted, and the mission was successfully performed. In July, 1778, the whole population of the village went to the church in a body and took the oath of allegiance to the United States. Capt. Leonard Helm was then sent by Clark to take charge of the post and make friends of the Indians of the vicinity. He made formal alliance with the

Piankeshaws, and, with a small force, ascended the Wabash to Post Ouiatenon, frightened away the British agent, and made a treaty with the Indians there.

This American occupation was short-lived. In the fall of the same year Lieut.-Gov. Hamilton came down the Wabash with a force of 80 white men and 400 Indians, and on Dec. 15 appeared at Vincennes. Helm had but one man in the fort with him, but was allowed to surrender with the honors of war, and the Wabash was again under British control. As soon as Clark learned of this he began active preparations for the recapture of the post, for he knew that if he waited until spring Hamilton would be reinforced by Indians, and probably by troops, and he would be helpless. On Feb. 5, 1779, he started across the flooded prairies of Illinois at the head of 170 men, armed only with rifles and with scanty supplies, to capture the stockade fort at Vincennes, garrisoned by 80 men, and supplied with several small cannon. Nineteen days elapsed before they reached Vincennes after a march of unexampled hardship, wet much of the time to the skin, their clothing at times frozen upon them, and the last five days practically without food. On the evening of the 23d of February the attack was begun, and pressed with such spirit that on the next evening Hamilton agreed to surrender. The capitulation was made on the morning of Feb. 25, Vincennes passed finally into American hands, and the power of the British on the Wabash was broken forever. Thereafter the post was the extreme of the American frontier in the contest that was waged with the Indians for the following sixteen years.

It was not a pleasant period anywhere on the frontiers, and it was a depressing period to the people of Vincennes, although there was no fighting in its immediate vicinity. All trade was cut off with Canada, and that down the Mississippi was made very dangerous by the southern Indians, who had also espoused the British cause. Supplies at Vincennes advanced four or five hundred per cent. in price, and it was charged that merchants took advantage of the situation to enrich themselves to the public detriment. By the ordinance of 1787 all this region was included in the territory northwest of the Ohio river, and government was established in what is now Ohio, but it was not actually extended over the French settlements until 1790. Meanwhile Vincennes was under military rule, and Major Hamtramck, who was in command, had the good sense to exercise the despotic powers of a French commandant. He prohibited absolutely the sale of liquor to the Indians, and saved the simple French settlers from the wiles of American adventurers by forbidding the sale or mortgage of real or personal property without his consent. But under his rule new misfortunes came. Unusual floods did great damage, and unprecedented frosts killed the crops. In 1790 actual famine prevailed at Vincennes and if relief had not been sent from the American settlements many must have perished. There was little relief from the adverse conditions till the close of the Indian hostilities with Wayne's victory in 1795.

After Hamtramck's rule there was no restriction on trade, and many of the French, pinched by poverty and improvident in character, parted with their valuable land claims for little or nothing, before the lands were allotted, to Americans who were waiting to buy. The Americans were quickly in the ascendency in all political matters. When Gen. Harmar came to the post in 1787 he estimated the population at 900 French and 400 Americans, and of course the proportion of adult males among the latter was very much the greater. In 1796, when Volney visited the old post, he found the French settlers in a dispirited frame of mind. They considered themselves downtrodden and oppressed, but aside from what advantage was taken of them by individuals there was no particular cause for this complaint. They were simply coming under a new form of government which they did not understand, and for which they were not very well fitted. The paternal care of the commandant was taken

away, and they were left to look out for themselves. Of self-government they knew nothing, and they cared nothing for it. In fact there was not much self-government in this period, for only one election was held—that for delegates to the territorial assembly of 1799. The laws and customs of the Americans were new to them, and American theories of government were entirely foreign to them. Nevertheless they were good citizens and accommodated themselves to the new system as graciously as possible, and in due time their descendants became as thoroughly American as any of their neighbors.

THE TERRITORIAL PERIOD.

The government of Indiana territory was inaugurated with William Henry Harrison as governor, John Gibson, secretary, and William Clark, Henry Vanderburgh and John Griffin as judges. At least such were the appointments, but the only official on the ground was the secretary, for Harrison did not arrive till Jan. 10 of the next year, and no court was held until March following. The government was the customary territorial government of the first stage, with the legislative power vested in the governor and judges. A session of this body was held immediately after Harrison's arrival, but there was not much legislation needed, for as a legislative body they decided that the laws of Northwest territory were in force in Indiana territory, and as executive and judiciary they held likewise. The laws of Northwest territory were very well adapted to Indiana territory, and so this course was very satisfactory.

The great work of the territorial period was clearing the land and bringing it under cultivation. Nature was to be subdued first. Of course there was a social development coincident with this physical change of the state, and political contests that were of temporary interest at least. The great question of the territorial period was pretty well under consideration when the territory was formed, and occupied general attention from the beginning. It was the question of the introduction of slavery into Indiana. The clause in the ordinance of 1787 prohibiting slavery in the territory northwest of the Ohio had never been enforced literally. Slavery had existed there up to the time of the ordinance, and that instrument plainly guaranteed to the citizens of the region their property and also their "laws and customs" relative to the descent and conveyance of property. Gov. St. Clair was of the opinion that no interference with the slavery already existing was contemplated, and the courts and the people coincided with his view, so the slavery continued as before. But many of the French settlers, before this conclusion was reached, alarmed by the possibility of losing their slaves, had moved across the Mississippi, or had sent their slaves out of the territory. Some of these desired to return and some wanted to bring their slaves back, but that was prohibited by the ordinance without question. Even a petition to the legislature of Northwest territory from Virginia soldiers to bring their slaves into the military grants given them north of the Ohio was promptly refused as inconsistent with the ordinance.

The French settlers had not accepted the prohibition of slavery without protest. In 1796 a petition had been sent to congress from the Illinois country, where slavery was most prevalent, signed by four of the leading men of that region on behalf of the inhabitants. It urged that the prohibition was contrary to the promises made to them by Gen. Clark, destructive of vested rights, and imposed on them as a "compact" when they had never consented to it. They also urged that slavery was essential to the welfare of the region because labor was so scarce and dear that even unskilled labor could not be had at less than a dollar a day. Congress promptly disposed of this request on the ground that it had but four signers, and that other residents would object to any change in the ordinance as to slavery, which was very true of those in the region east of the Miami. The ruling of the territorial authorities gave some assurance to the people as to slaves already held in the territory, but the desire to bring in others grew. In 1800 another petition was sent up from the Illinois country, with 270 signatures, asking a modification of the slavery clause which would allow the importation of slaves from the states, but providing that the children of such slaves should be free at the age of twenty-eight years for females and thirty-one years for males. This petition was simply laid on the table.

The theory on which slavery was maintained in the territory is set out in the following opinion rendered by one of the best lawyers then in this region, in the case of a negress who was afterwards set free, in 1820, by a decision of the Supreme court, which held that slavery was prohibited by the state constitution of Indiana:

OPINION OF JOHN JOHNSON, IN POLLY'S CASE.

"In 1779 or '80 a negro woman was taken prisoner by the Indians, of the age of 15. She was sold to Isaac Williams, at Detroit, and sold by said Williams to Antoine Lasselle. While the said woman was in the possession of Lasselle she had three children, two of whom I. B. Laplant purchased. Question, are those children slaves?

As to the first point, the woman was taken by the Indians as allies of England while they were in a state of warfare with the state of Virginia and the other states of the United States. As such she must be considered as a lawful prize, at least so much so that the conqueror had a right by virtue of his power to dispose of her life or person as he might think proper. This position is strengthened because of her being held as a species of property by her owner before and at the time she was taken. Secondly Detroit and what was formerly called the Northwestern territory in the year 1779 and '80 (nay until 1783) was an integral part of the state of Virginia and governed by the same laws. By a law of the colony of Virginia passed in the year 1705 negroes reduced to possession are considered as slaves. This law still continues in force with some small variation with regard to the manner of transferring that property. Thus the said woman could be held

15

as a slave either by virtue of conquest or by virtue of the laws of Virginia.

In 1783 Virginia ceded the Northwestern territory including Detroit to the United States. By the articles of cession and by the ordinance for the government of this territory the rights and privileges and also the property of the inhabitants are guaranteed to them. Hence the said negro woman being taken and considered as a species of property prior to the adoption of the ordinance for the government of the said territory the 6th article thereof which prohibits involuntary servitude can not affect her condition or the rights of her master. Thirdly the children follow the condition of the mother and not of the father. This point is as well defined by law as any other whatever and the reason of it is this. The slave being considered as the absolute property of the master for life he has a right to all the undivided emoluments arising from such slave and the increase of such female slave being part of the benefit arising from such kind of property as much so as her labor. From the foregoing premises I am decidedly of opinion that the children of the negro woman alluded to are slaves.   JNO. JOHNSON."

When Harrison arrived a movement was already on foot for an immediate advance to the second grade of territorial government so that the people would have a representative in congress, who could get some attention for their demands. This could be done at once if Harrison were willing, for the division act provided that the second-grade should be in force "whenever satisfactory evidence shall be given to the governor thereof that such is the wish of a majority of the freeholders." Sufficient signed petitions were presented to the governor, but he did not desire the change, which would lessen his political power, and put in print a letter giving an estimate of the heavy taxation that would be caused by the change, whereby public sentiment was reversed, and most of the petitioners were glad to have no action taken. But the demand for the introduction of slavery was not at all abated, and in 1802 Gov. Harrison expressed his willingness to call a convention to consider the matter if petitioned so to do. Petitions were put in circulation, but on Nov. 22, without waiting for their presentation, the governor called an election to be held on Dec. 11, and directed the delegates to assemble at Vincennes on Dec. 20. There were three delegates each from Randolph and St. Clair counties, which covered the Illinois settlements, four from Knox county, which included southwestern Indiana, and two from Clark county, which included the southeastern part of Indiana. All of the delegates except those from Clark county favored the admission of slavery. The convention organized by electing Gov. Harrison president, and prepared a memorial to congress asking suspension of the ordinance provision against slavery for the period of ten years. It also asked for pre-emption rights to public lands, for land grants for schools and in aid of the construction of roads, and other privileges. The memorial was laid before the house of representatives on Feb. 8, 1803, and referred to a committee of which John Randolph of Roanoake was chairman. It favored granting some of the requests, but emphatically opposed allowing the introduction of slavery, and urged that the prohibition was a "sagacious and benevolent restraint." No further action was taken at this session, but on Dec. 15, 1803, the matter was referred to a new committee which reported favorably to a suspension of the slavery clause for ten years. No action by congress was taken on this report.

The people of the western part of the territory were much displeased by the failure of congress to grant their requests, and were determined to have slavery whether or no. On Sept. 22, 1803, the governor and judges adopted a law providing for slavery by apprenticeship, or, as it was worded, that a person coming into the territory "under contract to serve another in any trade or occupation shall be compelled to perform such contract specifically during the term thereof." It made no distinction as to color, except that if a negro or an

Indian should "presume to purchase a white servant," such servant should become free. This law was in violation of the ordinance in several respects, but slaves were imported under its provisions. In this year the Illinois people showed their desire to get rid of the ordinance by petitioning congress to be added to Louisiana, but congress did not heed the request. It did provide, however, that the governor and judges of Indiana should make laws for the district of Louisiana, and this power was exercised for about one year, after which it was given a separate territorial government.

There was dissatisfaction all around. The people of Michigan, which constituted Wayne county in the territory, were demanding a separate territorial government on account of the inconvenience of having the seat of government at so great a distance. The people of Clark county and those of Dearborn county, which was constituted of the country lying between Ohio and the Greenville treaty line, were dissatisfied with the slavery sentiments of the administration. The rest of the people were dissatisfied with the law for slavery by apprenticeship, which was clearly illegal because it was not taken from the laws of any of the states as required by the ordinance, and because a contract made under duress was void. Harrison concluded that the best course was to go to the second grade. A form of election to ascertain the wishes of the people was held, at which very few votes were cast, and on Dec. 5, 1804, the governor made proclamation that Indiana territory had advanced to the second grade of territorial government. He also called an election for legislators to be held on Jan. 3, 1805, apportioning three delegates to Wayne county, two to Knox, and one each to Dearborn, Clark, Randolph and St. Clair. Michigan was made a separate territory before the legislature met, and so the Wayne county people had no part in it.

The first business of the legislature was the election of a congressman. It chose Benjamin Parke, who was a member of the governor's party, and a most excellent man. It next passed an act for the introduction of negroes to the territory. It allowed the slaveholders to bring them in, and within thirty days to make a contract for service for a term of years, which should be enforcible. If the slave refused to make a contract he could be removed from the territory. The children of these "apprentices" were required to serve, if males, until thirty-five years of age, and if females, until thirty-two. A petition to congress for the suspension of the slavery clause was brought before the legislature, but it was not adopted. The members who favored it, however, signed it as members "constituting a majority of the two houses respectively," and forwarded it to congress. This petition was designed to counteract two others, one of which had been sent to congress from the Illinois country asking the introduction of slavery, but denouncing the Harrison administration, and asking the separation of Illinois. The other was from Dearborn county asking that it be reannexed to Ohio. These petitions, together with all preceding ones, were referred by congress to a special committee of seven, which on Feb. 14, 1806, reported in favor of suspending the slavery clause for ten years, and against division of the territory. No action on the report was taken by the house. On March 26 two more petitions from the Illinois country for division and the introduction of slavery were presented, which were referred to the same committee and there remained.

The Indiana legislature met again on Nov. 3, 1806, and the pro-slavery people laid aside their differences on the question of dividing the territory long enough to agree on a petition for the suspension of the slavery clause, which was duly sent to congress. But there was not the same agreement outside. The anti-Harrison people in the Illinois country sent in a petition for division and slavery, and the Harrison people sent in one for slavery but against division. The committee of congress to which they were all referred reported favorably to the suspension of the slavery clause and against division, but no action was taken on the report.

In 1807 a new legislature was elected, but it differed little in sentiment from the preceding one, except that the anti-slavery men were a little more obstinate in their position. The legislature re-elected Benjamin Parke to congress, and re-enacted the apprentice law with very slight modifications. It also adopted a memorial to congress for suspension of the slavery clause. By this time the anti-slavery people were wakened to the necessity for action. In Clark county a public meeting was held and resolutions opposing the suspension of the slavery clause were adopted. These resolutions first declared the doctrine of "Squatter Sovereignty," and asked congress not to interfere until the territory was ready for statehood, when the people should be allowed to decide the question for themselves. From Dearborn county a petition was sent denouncing the apprentice law as a violation of the ordinance and asking to be reannexed to Ohio. These petitions were referred to committees in both houses. The senate committee reported that it was inexpedient to suspend the slavery clause, and the house committee took no action.

In 1808 a change occurred in the legislature. Two members of the house from Randolph and St. Clair counties had been appointed to the council. They were both Harrison men. A special election was called to fill the vacancies, and after a bitter contest the anti-Harrison faction triumphed in both counties. When the legislature assembled the anti-Harrison pro-slavery members made a combination with the anti-slavery members. They elected Jesse B. Thomas to congress. Numerous petitions for and against slavery were presented to the legislature. They were referred to a committee of which General W. Johnston was chairman, and he made a memorable and very able report against the introduction of slavery, and for the repeal of the apprentice laws, for which purpose he presented a bill. The house concurred in the report and passed the repeal bill, but it was defeated by the council five days later. This action was communicated to congress to-

gether with resolutions asking that the representative in congress be made elective by the people. There were also several petitions sent in for the division of the territory. The house committee, of which Thomas was chairman, reported favorably to division, and a bill for that purpose was adopted Feb. 3, 1809. The committee estimate the population of the territory west of the Wabash, at that time, at 11,000, and those east of the Wabash at 17,000. Thomas also secured a law making the representative in congress and the members of the legislative council elective by the people, and giving the power of legislative apportionment to the legislature.

This action reduced Indiana territory to practically the present limits of the state, though at that time only about one-fourth of the state, the lower part, was settled. The remainder was held by the Indians. Politics took a new form. The Harrison party put forward Thomas Randolph as a candidate for congress. Against him appeared Jonathan Jennings, a youth of 25 years, who was a native of New Jersey, and had lived for three years in the territory. It was an exciting campaign. Randolph tried to evade the slavery issue by promising to be controlled by the wishes of his constituents on that subject. Jennings stood flatly against slavery. Sentiment was pretty evenly divided, and the situation was complicated by the candidacy of John Johnson, of Knox county. The election resulted: Jennings 428, Randolph 402, Johnson 81. The Harrison party were very sore over this defeat, and also over the fact that the legislature elected at the same time was against them. The point was raised that the election was illegal because there had been no apportionment after the division act was adopted, and the whole matter was submitted to congress. It held that the legislature was illegal, and the house committee reported likewise as to the election of a representative, but no further action was taken in that matter. Another legislature was elected in 1810, with a small but determined anti-slavery majority. It made its session memorable by repealing the apprentice law, but saved the rights and liabilities that had accrued under it. In 1811 another election for congress was held, with Jennings and Randolph as candidates, and the former was successful. This was the decisive defeat of the pro-slavery party in Indiana, and it was so recognized. Its leaders tried to escape the odium of its advocacy by declaring it finally and irrevocably settled, but Jennings would not let it rest, and continued to make free soil campaigns. His party grew stronger daily, for population was coming in rapidly, and slave-holders were not among them. He was easily elected in 1812 over Waller Taylor, and in 1814 over Elijah Sparks. In 1816, under the enabling act, an anti-slavery constitutional convention was elected, and the question was finally disposed of in our politics.

It would be unjust to leave this subject without mention of the physical conditions that were largely the cause of the early pro-slavery sentiment. The heavy forest that covered Indiana was a great obstacle in the eyes of the pioneers. Who was to clear it away? Men who were wealthy enough to own more land than sufficed for family needs were not going to chop wood. Men of small means could get land of their own, and would rather clear it than work for others. The first petition from the territory called attention to the scarcity of labor and the fact that it could not be procured "under one dollar per day." There was practically no market for the timber after it was cut. What was not used for buildings and rails was burned. Who was to clear the land? Even the Dearborn county people, when petitioning for reannexation in Ohio in 1805, spoke of the land lying between them and Vincennes as "a wilderness occupy'd only by Indians and likely for many years to remain unoccupied by any other persons." And yet in fifteen years that part of the state was comparatively well settled, and people who were living at that time lived to see the day when warnings began to be uttered against the destruction of the forests. The century has not yet passed, but the state

has enacted laws to promote the planting and preservation of forest trees. Who could foresee this when only two or three thousand people had located just within the borders of the state and stood confronting the vast, unbroken forest that stretched out before them? It was the homeseeker who removed it—the man who came to the wilds to establish an abiding place for himself and his children. Foot by foot, mile by mile, they cut into the wilderness, and every foot that was gained was held by these people who had come to be a part of the new commonwealth. And much of the greatness of the commonwealth is due to this fact of its building by men whose object in life was to make homes—men who were willing to toil, to endure privations, and to wait. It is a commonwealth of homes, where homes are appreciated and loved, and where people are always ready for advances that will makes homes better and happier.

There was not much of interest in the politics of the territory, after the slavery question was disposed of as a practical issue. The people were more engrossed with war matters. The trouble with the Indians, which resulted in the battle of Tippecanoe, was in 1811. Randolph was killed at that battle. The echoes of it had not passed away when the war of 1812 came on, and the militia from the west pressed north to Detroit and on into Canada. Harrison was with the army, and his place was filled in 1813 by the appointment of Gen. Thomas Posey as governor. He was not a forceful man, though he had held several high positions. At this time he was advanced in years and not in robust health. He performed the functions of his office, but left no impress on the territory over which he continued to preside while it was a territory, which was but three years. It was a period of rapid growth. In 1810 the population of the territory was 24,520. In 1815, when the enabling act was passed, the population, the free white population, was found by special census to be 63,897. There were at that time thirteen organized counties in the territory. Agriculture was the great industry, but there was some manufacturing in simpler forms. In 1810 there were in the territory 33 grist mills, 14 saw mills, 3 horse mills, 18 tanneries, 28 distilleries, 3 powder mills, 1,256 looms and 1,356 spinning wheels. The value of manufactures in that year was about $200,-000, chiefly of homespun fabrics made by the pioneer women. Facilities for transportation were defective. Roads were not numerous, and not good. Steamboat navigation was as yet only experimental on western waters. The only market for the products of the territory was New Orleans, which was reached by flat-boats and barges. There was not much encouragement to raise surplus products, and it has been estimated that, in 1816, on seven-eighths of the farms in the state the cultivated land did not exceed from five to twenty acres, chiefly in cornfields. The people had their homes and their living, and they were not disturbed by any wild dreams of ambition and splendor.

EARLY YEARS OF THE STATE.

The first election under the state constitution resulted in the choice of Jonathan Jennings for governor and Christopher Harrison for lieutenant-governor. William Hendricks, who had been secretary of the constitutional convention, was elected representative in congress. The remaining state officers were elected by the legislature, and also the two senators, James Noble and Waller Taylor. This elective power of the legislature was not felt to be an evil at that time, though it afterward became so. The same may be said of several other powers lodged in the legislature, such as the granting of divorces and granting franchises by special acts. The constitution was, however, a very satisfactory basic law for the times and served its purpose well. The state began its existence auspiciously. For several years good health prevailed and immigration was rapid. It was just about with the organization of the state government that steamboat transportation began to develop on the western rivers. There had been some experiments before that time,

but nothing of practical importance. In 1817 Mr. Birkbeck estimated that there were about 25 steamboats on the Mississippi and its tributaries, and predicted that they were destined to become of much importance to the western people. They were able to make about 60 miles a day against the current. He gives the log of the Etna on a trip from New Orleans to Louisville, leaving the former on June 6, and arriving at its destination on July 14. It passed 8 barges and 7 steamboats on the trip. The rates for transportation from New Orleans to Louisville at that time were $125 for a passage and $112 a ton for freight. They were reduced in 1819. The rates down stream were one-half. By 1820 there had been 71 steamboats built on western rivers, and about 200 more were added by 1830. Between 1830 and 1840 there were 729 steamboats built on the western rivers.

The development of steamboat transportation made very good markets along the navigable waters. Along the Ohio flour sold at $7 to $8 a barrel; corn at 30 to 50 cents a bushel, and pork at 10 to 15 cents a pound. Skilled mechanics received from $1.50 to $2.00 per day and common laborers about one-half that rate. Government land was sold at $2 an acre, one-fourth down, and as it was rising rapidly in value much profit was made by paying the entrance money and selling to newcomers at an advance. Immigration was so rapid that in 1820 the population had reached 147,178. The southern end of the state was becoming too crowded for the expansive pioneers, and there was a demand for more room. In 1818 Gov. Jennings, with Gov. Cass and Judge Parke, were appointed commissioners to treat with the Indians, and succeeded in purchasing all the territory south of the Wabash except a few reservations. This gave ample room for new settlers for a time, but a queer complication arose from it. The constitution of the state prohibited the governor from holding "any office under the United States," and the governor had obviously violated it. The arrangments for the treaty had been kept secret, to insure its success, but as soon as Lieutenant-Governor Harrison learned of the situation he took possession of the governor's office, on the theory that Jennings had vacated it, and refused to surrender possession on his return. When the legislature assembled both houses recognized Harrison as governor, but appointed a committee to investigate the matter. It reported in favor of Jennings and the legislature adopted the report by a majority of two. Harrison at once resigned as lieutenant-governor, and in 1819 became a candidate for governor against Jennings, but the people were against him also, and Jennings was re-elected by an emphatic vote of 9,168 to 2,088.

The opening prosperity of the state was destined to a serious reverse. The years 1820, 1821 and 1822 were marked by widespread and fatal sickness. The ague and intermittent fevers common to the state in its early development took on an aggravated form, and were accompanied by an epidemic of a bilious fever that resembled yellow fever in symptoms and in violence. Medical aid was not common enough or adequate enough for such an emergency, and the loss of life was very heavy. It was estimated that many of the towns lost one-eighth of their population in 1820, and one-fourth in the three years. A serious financial crisis came on at the same time. During the war of 1812 specie payments had been universally suspended, and, as is universally the case under such conditions, paper money was issued to an unjustifiable extent. But it made "good times," and times were kept good temporarily by issuing more paper money. The financial interests of the country insisted on a return to specie payments, and in 1816 congress chartered the United States bank with a capital of $35,000,-000, to issue notes convertible at all times into gold and silver. As its notes came into circulation those of the banks that did not resume, and most of the western banks did not, necessarily circulated at a discount, and payment could be made in them only at market rates. In other words the standard of value as to deferred payments was raised, and the deferred payments in the west were large in amount. In 1814 the territorial legislature of Indiana had chartered two banks, the Bank of Vincennes and the Farmers' and Mechanics' bank of Madison, both of which were authorized to issue notes. They were managed with some prudence at first, but later with a recklessness which, in the case of the former at least, could scarcely be distinguished from criminality. The constitution of 1816 prohibited the legislature from chartering any bank to issue circulating notes except a state bank, but preserved the charter rights of the two banks mentioned. In 1817 the Bank of Vincennes was made a state bank, with power to establish branches, and to adopt the Madison bank as one of its branches. It began issuing notes with great freedom. The notes of banks of adjoining states, of no better standing, were also freely circulated, and in addition to this many business men issued notes, especially of small denominations, which were circulated as currency. The crash began to be felt in 1819, and progressed rapidly. In 1821 the legislature ordered proceedings to cancel the charter of the Bank of Vincennes on account of mismanagement, and its failure was as discreditable as could be imagined. Most of the paper of it and its branches became worthless in the hands of holders, though that of the Madison branch was ultimately redeemed after circulating at a discount for some years. The general government, which had over $200,000, proceeds of land sales, on deposit in the Bank of Vincennes, lost nearly all of it.

But this was not the worst. There had been an era of speculation, especially in lands and in the lots of projected towns, and men had strained their credit to the utmost. Payment was hopeless, and the number of debtors to the government was so great that absolute enforcement of their liabilities was out of the question. A compromise solution was adopted by the congress of 1821. It released all claims for interest—which then amounted to about one-third of the total land debt, and allowed lands on which part payments had been made to be relinquished and the money to be credited against other lands in full payment. It also reduced the price of lands from $2 to $1.25 per acre, and required that all lands thereafter should be paid for in full in cash. This of course made a great reduction in the current value of land, though not perhaps greater than the increase in value of the money standard from the old bank notes to the new specie standard. From 1820 to 1825 the prices of all kinds of produce were from one-third to one-fourth of what they had been, but the people did not realize that this was due to a change of the money by which they were measured. The collection of debts by law involved vast sacrifice of former, and indeed of actual values, and in consequence relief laws to obstruct the collection of debts were passed. "Hard times" had come and made themselves felt. As is always the case, they begot economy and caution in business, and these, together with the great natural resources of the state and continued immigration started the people in the up-grade once more. From 1826 to 1834 there was a gradual though not large advance of prices, and a gradual restoration of prosperity. Notwithstanding the bad conditions of the first half of the decade, the population in 1830 advanced to 343,031.

Most of the lessons of this period were either not understood or soon forgotten, but one had a permanent effect. The people saw the necessity for a stable currency and safe banking. Out of the reflection on their experience and the study of their necessities the backwoods financiers evolved a plan for a state banking system which enjoys the honor of being admitted by students of finance to-day to be the most successful one ever known in this country. It was for a state bank with a capital of $1,600,000, of which the state took one-half. It issued bonds for $1,300,000 which it sold abroad, and the proceeds were used first to pay for its share of the stock, and the remaining $500,000 to loan at 6 per cent. to individual purchasers of stock to aid them in paying. The

individual who bought stock paid three-eights down and five-eights with money borrowed from the state. His share of profits was credited on this debt until it was extinguished, and that was soon done. The branches and main bank were eventually responsible for redemption of notes, but each had its own profits. No loan of over $500 could be made without the consent of five of the seven directors of a branch, and no loan of over $5,000 could be made without consent of the main bank. The bank could issue bills, and was forbidden to suspend specie redemption. It was forced to do so, however, in the panic of 1837, but its notes depreciated very slightly, and it resumed in 1842 without loss to anybody. The bank was an absolute monopoly, and was subject to no tax except an annual state tax of 25 cents on each $100 of stock. All the profits of the state, with the repaid money advanced to shareholders, were carried to a sinking fund, under charge of special commissioners, which was devoted primarily to the payment of the state's bank bonds, with interest on the same, and the residue to a permanent common school fund. Both bank and sinking fund were so well managed that at the closing up of the bank's affairs the state had accumulated profits of more than $3,000,000, which formed the chief basis of the present splendid school fund of the state. But more important than this, the bank supplied the people with a reliable currency and safe banking facilities for a quarter of a century, and bred a class of bankers who were both useful and creditable to the state in after years.

The politics of the state at this time was of a local and personal character, the Jennings party being strongly ascendant. Jennings was elected for two terms, of three years each, as governor, which was all the constitution allowed. He resigned shortly before the close of the second term, having been elected to congress. He continued in congress until 1831, and died in 1834. The usefulness of his later years was much impaired by intemperance. His unexpired term as governor was filled by the lieutenant governor Ratliff Boon, and in 1822 William Hendricks was elected governor. He was of the Jennings party and received all of the 18,340 votes cast, no candidate appearing against him. He served until February, 1825, when he resigned, having been elected United States senator. He was re-elected to the senate in 1831. As governor he was succeeded by James Brown Ray, president of the state senate. Mr. Ray was elected governor in the fall of 1825, and again in 1828, at the latter election defeating Dr. Canby, who ran as a Jackson man, and H. H. Moon, who ran as an Adams man. The vote stood Ray 15,141, Canby 12,315, and Moon 10,904. It is evident that national politics had no strong domination in Indiana at this time. The seat of territorial government had been transferred from Vincennes to Corydon, in Harrison county, in the year 1813, and the seat of state government was continued there. In 1820, congress having granted four sections of land to the state for a permanent capital, a commission was appointed which selected the present site of Indianapolis. The seat of state government was transferred to this point in 1825. The state at first made use of the Marion court house for the transaction of its business, having contributed $8,000 to the construction of that building on agreement that it should be used for legislative purposes for fifty years. But public needs soon outgrew its capacity and in 1832 provision was made for a state capitol, which was completed in 1837.

PIONEER CONDITIONS AND CUSTOMS.

Although the pioneer settlement of Indiana covered quite a long period there was a great deal of similiarity about it. The state was mostly covered by forest below the Wabash, and there was the same kind of work to be done by those who came to make homes, and they were largely the same kind of people. The process of subduing nature was much the same everywhere, and as it has best been told by those who lived through it, their statements will be freely quoted in this description. The first business of the settler, after making his location, was to cut off and remove all the large timber from a few acres upon which his cabin was to be built. Cabins in those early times were built entirely of round logs from eight to ten inches in diameter and of lengths to suit the builder, and were covered with clapboards. Where the family was large, cabins were in size about eighteen by twenty-five feet, one nine-foot story, with a rather low garret bedroom above; where the family was small the building was generally about eighteen feet square with garret room. Cabins generally had but one door and one window, but occasionally the larger-sized had two of each. The chimney and fireplace were always on the outside of the house, thus allowing the full internal dimensions for the use of the family. The material being made ready and placed on the ground where the building was to be erected, a day was fixed for the "raising." To this all the settlers for several miles around were invited and attended, it being understood that all were needed. There was no shirking: "Help me and I will help you"; "Refuse to help me and you are no neighbor, and you might as well leave." On the day thus appointed the cabin was generally raised and put under roof. Cutting out places for doors, windows and fireplace, putting in the doors and windows, building the fireplace and stick chimney, laying the puncheon floors, chinking and daubing up the cracks between the logs were done by the farmer at his pleasure. Log barns and outhouses were added as soon as it could be done without too much of a drain upon the industry of the neighbors. These log cabins were very plain structures, but were the best early settlers could possess themselves of, and when properly constructed, made a strong and tolerably comfortable place to live in, much warmer and more substantial than many of the frame houses of the present time. Into these humble dwellings did the settlers and their families enter, and for many years lived more contented and happy doubtless than many now living in elegant and costly stone fronts.

The next thing in order was for the settler

with all his available force, which frequently included his wife or daughter and sometimes both, to clear off an eligible piece of land upon which to plant a young orchard, all timber being removed from this piece. Here as soon as the trees could be procured was planted a small orchard. A few of these orchards, now more than half a century old, can still be seen standing, the hands that planted them having long since passed from earth, and the trees showing the damaging effects of time. This land was generally cultivated in corn or other crops for several years. The next thing in order in the clearing process was to deaden the timber upon a number of acres of the land to be improved, and then as fast as possible to clear up and put into cultivation as many acres each year as possible, this additional clearing being generally done by grubbing out all underbrush and cutting down all timber having a diameter of eighteen inches at a height of two feet from the ground and all of a less size, all brush being burned, and the logs cut into suitable lengths for heaping and burning. Generally several acres on each farm were thus prepared during the winter. When thus prepared a "log-rolling" was provided for and a day fixed to which all the neighbors were invited. Sometimes the good wife would have connected with the "log-rolling" a "bed-quilting," to which all the women folk were invited and attended. This was frequently the occasion of much merriment and real enjoyment, winding up with a jolly dance, commonly called a "hoe-down." Thus from time to time for several years as new settlers would come in and purchase pieces of heavily-timbered land, went on this routine of house-raisings, log-rollings, quiltings and dances. Corn husking, coupled with quiltings and winding up with dances, soon became an additional means of calling the settlers of both sexes together, particularly the younger.

This part of the country being so far interior and approached only through the wilderness, without roads, the early settlers were only able to bring with them such articles of furniture as they could not get along well without, and such as were light and not easily broken by the rough usage to which they would necessarily be subjected. Hence the household and kitchen furniture generally consisted of a reasonable supply of plain, substantial articles, embracing one or more feather beds with the requisite bedding, a substantial set of pewter ware, etc. The greatest deficiency was in bedsteads, tables and chairs, there being no cabinetmakers in the country, and no prepared material for them to work on had there been any. The first settlers were under the necessity of procuring these articles, or rather substitutes, for themselves, which they did in about this wise: For bedsteads an oak tree that would split well was selected, cut down, and a log about eight feet long taken from the butt and split into such pieces as could be readily shaped into posts and rails. Another log not so long was split into such pieces as with slight dressing made slats. Holes were bored with a tolerably large auger in suitable places in the posts for inserting the rails; two rails were used for each side, and about three for each end, the end rails answering for head and foot boards. Like auger holes were made in the lower side rails at suitable points for inserting the slats. When properly prepared this bedstead was put together by pressing the rails and slats in the holes prepared for each, thus making a rough but strong high-post bedstead, the posts at the top being tightly held together by rods prepared for the purpose, upon which curtains were to be hung. Thus was created a bedstead. Generally two of these were used in each of the larger-sized cabins, placed in the rear end of the cabin so as to stand lengthwise with the end wall, feet to feet, with a space of several feet between beds. Curtains made of fancy-colored calico were always hung upon these bedsteads, hiding from external view the deformities of the bedstead, presenting a rather neat appearance and making the beds quite private. Usually the old folks occupied one and the girls the other of these beds. For the boys and young men sleeping places were provided upstairs upon beds on the floor, there not being sufficient space between the floor and roof for bedsteads. A rough kind of cupboard was provided in all cabins by boring auger holes and driving strong wood pins in the logs in the most convenient corner and in such position that when boards (clapboards in the beginning) were placed upon them there were made rather convenient but not very sightly places upon which to put the dishes. Being always open to view, the tendency was to cleanliness. For tables, a large tree was cut down, and a log, the length desired for the table, was cut off and split into pieces (slabs) as thin as possible. These slabs were generally two feet in width and six feet in length; when dressed and made as thin and smooth as possible two were put together with strong cross pieces tightly pinned with wood pins, the whole set upon four strong legs, thus making a strong but rough table four feet in width and six feet in length, the size of the table being governed by the size of the family. For seats benches were made of the same material as the table, about fifteen inches wide, some the full length of the tables, others not longer than two feet each, standing upon four strong wood legs; these were provided in such numbers as were desired. This rough furniture necessarily continued in use until saw mills came into existence and cabinetmakers and chairmakers made their appearance in the land. Then the bedstead gave way to those of better style and finish, but the curtains were retained; the rough tables gave way to those more elegant and convenient, made by skilled workmen, and the benches and stools gave place to the current chair. Several years were required to bring about this change.

Much has been spoken and written about the sickly character of this country at the commencement of the settlement and for many years after, much of the alleged sickness being attributed to the log cabins in which families had to live, cook, eat and sleep in the same room, much more than was warranted or justified by the facts. On account of the malaria created by the decaying timber caused by clearing up the country, the annual decay of the rank growth of wild vegetation, turning up and exposing to the hot sun the new soil, and the undrained condition of the country, there was unavoidably some sickness of a malarial character here in early times, as there has been and will continue to be in all new countries having a rich and productive soil as this had; but the amount was not half as great as charged, nor was the fact that whole families lived, cooked, ate and slept, summer and winter, in the cabin with one room below and a garret bedroom above, the cause of the sickness when sickness did exist. The fact that the settlers by reason of their scanty house room were constantly brought into contact with the purified atmosphere, created by the heat of the fire necessarily used, protected them from the malarial diseases so much complained of; the truth is in those early times numbers of persons and families came to this new country from older states and thickly-settled neighborhoods where they had neighbors and associates and plenty of them, and who from habits of life were not suited to the changed condition in which they were placed by the removal. As a consequence they became disappointed, dissatisfied, and were seized with a constant desire to return to the country and place from which they came; in other words they became "homesick." No little of the alleged sickness consisted purely of this homesickness, and readily disappeared when the afflicted got back to the happy land from which they had so unwisely emigrated. Occasionally these unfortunates fretted and worried themselves into a real spell of sickness. As might have been expected, there was some sickness in those early times, which was doubtless aggravated by lack of proper medical treatment. This is probably why at times diseases became epidemic as has been noted in the years 1821, 1822 and 1823. Many of the physicians who first came amongst us seemed to be wholly ignorant of the malarial diseases peculiar to the country. They generally provided themselves with a goodly supply of the largest and most approved lancets and unmeasured quantities of English calomel. With these evidences of medical skill, a flaming sign, painted on a clapboard, was hung out, and as opportunity offered these men of science and great medical skill went forth first to take from the unfortunate patient all the blood that could be extracted from his veins without killing on the spot, and then dosed out calomel enough to kill the largest-sized gorilla, which the patient was required to take in doses indicated. He was to be kept confined in a close room so that not a breath of pure, cool air could fan his cheeks or kiss his lips, and was to have neither meat nor drink, warm water alone excepted. This practice, while it lasted, greatly aggravated disease. It killed quick but cured slow. It was far less skillful than that practiced by the Indian doctors. Happily this ignorance was not winked at and soon gave way to a more intelligent and health-restoring system, not, however, until some of those practicing it had justly subjected themselves to the soubriquet of "Death on the Pale Horse."

The great food staple of the early settlers was corn, and the first work after getting housed was to prepare for raising corn. At first the early mills in the country were hand mills, or as they were often called "mortars," in which the corn was pounded into powder, but it did not make very good corn meal. Of course corn was used freely in the milk, as it is now, and after it was ripe it was used a great deal in the shape of "lye-hominy," or "home-made hominy," as it is now often called. It was much used in this shape by the French settlers. Another common form of using ripe corn was to parch it and either eat the grains or grind them into powder, which was carried by travelers for food. Often it was almost the only food carried on hunting expeditions or Indian campaigns. There were some rude attempts at better mills. One of them located at "Conner's Station," some fifteen miles above Indianapolis on White river, is thus described:

"Mr. Bush, who was a Vermonter, and who had brought with him quite a variety of mechanical tools, procured from White river some stones, out of which he made two small mill stones, and then prepared the necessary woodwork for putting the same in running condition, and fastened the mill up to a hackberry tree on the west bank of the river, the motive power being a long beam operated by horse power, a rawhide rope being used for belting. This mill would produce from two to two and a half bushels of good meal per day, and answered an excellent purpose, not only of doing the necessary grinding for our neighborhood but for the settlers of this section, who had to come to our settlement to purchase corn. No toll was charged at this mill. All that was required was that each person should furnish his own horse. This was the first mill built in the New Purchase."

There were also rude mills known as "corn crackers," and before many years very fair mills, for grinding both wheat and corn, operated by water power. One of the chief reasons for locating Indianapolis where it is was the supposition that Fall creek would supply ample water power for milling purposes of various kinds.

The bread made from corn meal was of several kinds. First there was what was called the "dodger"; secondly the "pone," and thirdly the "johnny cake." The "dodger" was a kind of bread made of corn meal mixed with pure water, with a little salt in it, made into a stiff dough, then rolled by the hands of the good housewife, or one that was to become such, into a ball about the size of your hand, put together into a kind of oblong shape, and baked in an iron bake-oven—a kind of cooking utensil with which all early settlers had provided themselves, being in size about the circumference of a half bushel measure, and in depth about eight inches, with an iron cover or lid, which could be put on and taken off at pleasure, and so constructed as to hold quite a quantity of coals upon its top. Coals underneath and on top of this oven, taken from a well-prepared wood fire in an old fashioned fireplace, with which all cabins were provided, constituted the heating power with which this kind of baking was done. "Pone" consisted of a preparation of corn meal mixed with water, with some milk or cream, and a quantity of yeast, prepared in some way known to the cooks, made into a dough not so stiff as that for the "dodger" and placed in this same oven, where in a short time it would become light, or what was then so considered, and was then baked in the same manner as the "dodger," thus making a loaf about six inches in thickness, and of the full internal dimensions of the oven. The "johnny cake" consisted of a dough made of corn meal with some lard or butter in it, about six inches in width and one inch in thickness, and placed upon a board prepared for the purpose, about two feet in length and from eight to ten inches in width, the baking being done by locating this board lengthwise before the open fire so as to present the full front of the cake to the fire, and so near it that the heat would in a reasonable time thoroughly cook that side of the cake, and enable the cook to loosen the cake from the board and turn the other side to the fire, by which means the cake would soon become thoroughly cooked, thus producing, as I have always believed, the best bread ever made out of corn. The pone was considered the next best, but the dodger, being the most convenient and readily made, was most used.

But the early settlers did not live by bread alone, as there was an abundance of meat easily obtainable. The country was full of game, such as deer, turkeys and pheasants, all of which constituted a very savory meat, and were readily obtained by the skilled riflemen, and nearly all the male portion of the early settlers, even down to quite youthful lads, were skilled in the use of that weapon. There was also a sufficient supply of hogs for the times,—some brought with them by the settlers, and some procured from Indians, a few of whom followed farming rather than the chase, and hence had procured quite a number of semi-tame hogs, which when joined to those brought by the settlers, furnished an ample supply of pork and a live stock to start with. The woods in every direction were pretty well supplied with hogs which had strayed away from the Indians, and with their increase had become thoroughly wild. These hogs both tame and wild were called "elm-eaters," and were peculiarly suited to the times and condition of things as they existed. They were long-legged, long-bodied, had extremely long heads and noses, with short straight up ears, and would at this age present a sorry picture at a show of improved swine, but at the time answered a valuable purpose. The wild hogs could only be made available during "mast" years which, although occurring oftener then than now, did not occur every year, by reason of which many of these wild hogs lived to become three and four years old before they would become sufficiently fat to make it an object to hunt and kill them. They thus became fleet of foot and very savage, making their presence at times extremely unpleasant and dangerous to the hunter, who had frequently to take to the nearest available tree for safety. During the non-mast years these hogs lived upon various kinds of roots they found in the woods, which they obtained by rooting with the long noses above mentioned. The principal root upon which they thus subsisted was the sweet or slippery elm, of the bark and fibrous roots of which they (as are all hogs) were very fond. Hence the name "elm-eaters." There was no hog cholera in those times, nor any while the hogs of the country had plenty of woodland to range over—not in even the modern improved breeds. There was one disadvantage about this pork, however. When fattened on mast, particularly hickory and beech, the meat was very oily and sweet, would shrink largely in cooking, and owing to its oily nature would not make bacon to advantage. This meat, however, answered a valuable purpose in its time. The capture of these wild hogs, although attended with some danger, offered to the sportsman of that day a considerable amount of real enjoyment which the present generation of sportsmen can never appreciate or enjoy.

Fish, which abounded in great numbers, and of the very best kind, such as bass, salmon, pike, buffalo, redhorse, etc., in the rivers and all their tributary streams, and were easily captured at all seasons of the year, entered as largely as was desired into the food of the settlers. Potatoes were raised the first year of the settlement in considerable quantities and of the very best quality, the new soil being better adapted to their growth and perfection than that in long use. This valuable article soon entered and formed a part of the food supply. Owing to the rich and wild nature of the soil, wheat could not be grown to advantage for several years, hence for some time all flour used had to be brought from abroad, and was consequently very expensive—so much so that little was used. When used it was considered a great luxury. It may not be wholly out of place here to briefly describe the manner and by what means the cooking of the food, other than bread, was done in those early times. It was done somewhat in this wise: For the purpose of boiling, a stiff bar or rod of iron-wood (when iron could not be had) was placed in the chimney lengthwise across the fireplace, the end resting upon the outer walls, about midway from front to rear, upon which were placed several hooks made of small iron rods, or of wood when iron could not be obtained, and of different lengths, the whole being of sufficient height that the pots, or "stew-kettles" as they were sometimes called, when hung upon these hooks would swing free of the fire underneath; in these pots or kettles were all boiled victuals cooked. For the purpose of roasting meats a strong wooden pin was placed in the inner wall of the house immediately over the middle of the large open fireplace. The turkey or venison saddle (both of which were largely used), or other meat to be roasted, was fastened to the end of a small cord (wire when it could be had) of sufficient length so that when the other end was fastened to the pin in the wall the meat to be roasted would hang suspended immediately in front of the fire, and so near that the heat would soon cook the part near the fire, and by occasional turnings would soon become well cooked—a pan or dish of some kind being always underneath to receive the dropping grease or oil. Extraordinary accounts are given of the abundance of game. As an illustration, it is related that Robert Harding, who was a noted hunter about Indianapolis in its first years, in the year 1820, on one occasion pushed his canoe containing his hunting material from the mouth of Fall creek (near which he was living) up the river to a point about the fourth of a mile below where the bridge across White river on the Michigan road is situated, being about five miles north of Fall creek, from which point he started homeward about 10 o'clock P. M., and on his way home killed nine deer, all bucks, having determined that night to kill nothing but bucks. On another occasion, during the fall of the same year, he and his brother at a point near where the pork houses now stand, two or three blocks below Washington street, killed thirty-seven turkeys out of one flock. Robert killed twenty-five and his brother twelve. This kind of slaughter was not frequent, but the killing of three or four deer, a half dozen to a dozen turkeys and fifteen or twenty pheasants by a single person in a single day or night hunt (deer being mostly killed in the night time) was not infrequent.

Of clothing the pioneers usually brought enough with them to last for a year or so, but that was soon worn out. Next to a food supply, the industry of the settlers was directed to the production of the material out of which the future supply of clothing was to be manufactured; hence at a very early period, and as soon as sufficient land could be cleared, inclosed and made ready for the seed, near every farm house could be seen a growing flax patch. This flax, when fully grown, was pulled and spread upon the same ground to rot, which process was soon accomplished by the dampness occasioned by the rains and the nightly dews. When sufficiently rotted that the woody fiber could be readily broken and separated from the lint fiber, the whole was gathered up and after being dried was by the hands of the stronger of the male portion of the family broken by the use of a kind of improvised machine called a "flax-brake," whereby the woody fibers would become thoroughly broken and mostly removed from the lint fiber, the remainder being removed by the whole lint fabric undergoing a process called "skutching," the lint at the same time undergoing a softening process, preparing it for the hand of the spinstress. By the process of what was called "hackling" in vogue in those times, the tow was separated from the thread fiber, and by the use of the spinning wheel (the little wheel), in the handling of which the mothers and all daughters of sufficient age were skilled, the flax was made into a fine strong thread called warp, and the tow into a coarser thread used as "filling." When thus prepared, by the use of a handloom, it was woven into a fabric called tow-linen. This was used for summer wear to a considerable extent by both sexes—that by the females being generally colored to suit the taste of the wearer; that worn by the males was left uncolored. As a means for providing for winter apparel, all settlers that could do so provided themselves with a few sheep, from which they procured wool; and those who could not procure sheep managed to purchase wool, which the good mothers and daughters manufactured into rolls by the aid of a pair of hand-cards, particularly provided for the purpose and owned by most families. These rolls were soon spun into yarn by the same hands on what was called the "big wheel," making "filling," (sometimes used for knitting stockings), and when mixed with linen warp and woven, made an article called "linsey woolsey," which when suitably colored made a strong, warm and rather handsome article of female apparel, and was considerably used. This same woolen yarn, when woven in connection with cotton warp made what was called "jeans," and was used by the males, mostly the older class, and was generally colored, oftener butternut than blue. Some cotton goods such as cambrics, muslins were occasionally seen in the settle-

ments, and such were appropriately used by both sexes, but owing to their scarcity and consequent high price, their use was quite limited. The outer apparel of the male population, particularly the younger and more active, soon became buckskin. This material was frequently procured already tanned by purchase from the Indians, but more frequently by the party killing the deer, dressing and tanning the skin himself, and thus making it ready for the tailor. Usually the only articles of clothing made of this material were pantaloons and coats, called in these times "hunting shirts," being much in the shape and style, barring the neat fit, of the sack coat so much in use among the gentlemen of the present time. There being no professional tailors in the beginning of the settlement and for some considerable time after, and this material being rather difficult for the seamstresses to handle, the thread used in its manufacture being the sinews taken from the legs of the deer or a thread called "whang," prepared by cutting a long strip as small as possible, so as not to make it too weak for the purpose intended, a large needle and a shoemaker's awl being used in the sewing process, each person, old or young, having a sufficient skill, was under the necessity of making his own clothes. This was generally done in a strong, substantial manner and when skillfully performed presented a very genteel appearance.

It was soon found that this buckskin apparel was the very best that could have been devised for the country and times. It resisted the sting of the nettles, the bite of the rattlesnake, and the penetration of the cold, bleak winds of winter, and at that time was cheap and within the reach of all. This kind of clothing, as in fact all other, was made quite large, so that the wearer would feel free and easy in its use. The consequence of this was that at times in right cold weather the wearer would stand so close to the large log fire that, without being conscious of it, his pants would get so hot that when suddenly pressed to his person by a mischievous associate, the warmth would cause him to leap clear across the room under the impression that the great log fire had fallen upon him. Another peculiarity attached to this kind of pantaloons was that when wet and allowed to dry without constant rubbing, they became quite hard and remained in the shape last left, and could not again be used until made soft by dampening. Indian-made moccasins, which were abundant and cheap, were much worn by both sexes (particularly the younger and more active class) in dry weather both winter and summer, being very comfortable and pleasant to the feet and presenting a rather neat appearance. For wet weather strong, well made leather shoes were used. Bare feet were quite as seldom seen then as now. The head dress for the male population for winter use consisted mostly of a strong, well made wool hat, with a low, broad brim, something in the style of the hat in use by the elder of the Quakers at this time. A rather unsightly but very warm kind of fur cap was used by some made out of a well-prepared coon skin. For summer wear, a rather rough homemade straw hat was made out the straw of rye, which was considerably grown for that purpose, the hat being very much in appearance and style of similar hats now in use. The female head dress consisted in part of a straw bonnet made of the same kind of straw and in part of a sunbonnet generally made out of some kind of fancy-colored calico worked over a stiff pasteboard; both straw and sunbonnets being of a style then in use, and of such shape and construction as to protect both the face and neck from the hot rays of the summer sun and the cold blasts of the winter winds. While there was very little money in circulation among the settlers, there was a valuable substitute to those who availed themselves of it, consisting of the fur skins of the raccoon and muskrat and the skin of the deer, all of which animals were quite plenty. A good deer skin taken in its season was worth fifty cents; that of a raccoon thirty-seven and a half cents, and that of the muskrat twenty-five cents, in trade —the proper season for taking the deer with

a view to the value of the skin being from about May 1st to the middle of November; that of the raccoon and muskrat from December 1st to April 1st. There was, therefore, but a very small portion of the year that the skilled hunter and trapper could not in that way and without any considerable loss of time procure means by which to furnish himself and his family, if he had one, with such articles of merchandise as were necessary and as the stores of that early day could furnish. All seemed to have had enough, when properly used, to answer reasonable wants. It should be added that the labor of the pioneer settlers, both men and women, was very severe. It has been observed by investigators that the majority of the men died under fifty years of age, having fully worn themselves out in the hard labor of chopping, rolling logs and grubbing out roots. Nevertheless, it had many compensations, and those who lived through it to the more comfortable times of more civilized surroundings always looked back with a sort of longing to the privations and privileges of the wilder life and its battle with nature.

THE INTERNAL IMPROVEMENTS.

There are few things connected with the history of Indiana as to which there is more misunderstanding than the internal improvement movement. That it was in a large sense a failure is true, but it has also come to be regarded as a peculiar epidemic of lunacy, which is absurdly untrue. As a matter of historical truth the people of one epoch are about as sensible as those of another, when the conditions and circumstances are all considered. There are of course instances of the prevalence of strange delusions, but these are seldom of long duration. There was nothing unreasonably hasty or impulsive about the internal improvement enterprise in Indiana. It was the result of years of consideration and discussion. Everybody at all familiar with the extent of our territory knew that there must be a provision of ways for transportation, and it seemed certain that the government must provide them. George Washington had started in 1774 the movement which resulted in the Chesapeake and Ohio canal, and the Cumberland road, commonly known in the west as "the National road," was begun in 1806. There was no party difference as to the necessity of improvements by governmental aid, though Jefferson, Madison and Monroe all opposed undertaking federal works that crossed the states, and this objection was finally met by constructing the national road under compacts with the states. It was realized from the first that it was unjust to allow federal revenues to be used for improving harbors and making coast defenses for the seaboard states if nothing were done for the interior states, and the war of 1812 demonstrated that the provision of means of transportation to the frontiers was a military necessity for the defense of the nation. After its close the sentiment throughout the country for internal improvements was very strong. John C. Calhoun was as ardent an advocate of them as Henry Clay. The absorbing questions were as to location and benefits.

When Indiana was admitted as a state, in 1816, a provision was put in the enabling act that 5 per cent. of the proceeds of all public lands sold in the territory should be reserved as a fund for the construction of roads and canals, and that three-fifths of this should be expended under the direction of the legislature of the state. This constituted what is known in our history as the "three per cent fund." In 1821 an appropriation was made from it for various state roads named in the act; in 1824 another for the improvement of the Wabash river, which was undertaken conjointly with Illinois; in 1830 one to aid the New Albany and Vincennes turnpike, etc. In 1827 congress made a special grant of lands in aid of the Wabash and Erie canal, and by acts of 1828 and 1830 the legislature of Indiana authorized its construction. The governors of the state favored internal improvements—they probably would not have been governors if they had not. Gov. Hendricks in 1822 urged husbanding the re-

sources of the state for the great work that must be done. Gov. Ray was an active supporter of the policy. He not only urged it in his messages of 1826, 1827 and 1829, but also in the "New Purchase" treaty of 1826 he obtained a reservation of a large quantity of land to aid in the construction of a road from Lake Michigan through Indianapolis to Madison, afterwards known as "the Michigan road." Gov. Noah Noble, who succeeded Gov. Ray in 1831, and was re-elected in 1834, was an ardent champion of internal improvements, and was elected largely on that account. The question pressing for settlement in his second term was whether the credit of the state should be used in aid of the works, and if so for what works. Very careful surveys and estimates of cost of construction of the principal proposed improvements had been made by expert engineers. The people had been addressed in newspapers, pamphlets and speeches. Naturally everybody wanted a part of the improvements in his vicinity, for the value of land and farm products varied inversely with the distance from a transportation route, and the cost of supplies the reverse. At every legislative session there was a shower of bills for roads and improvements, and it was evidently necessary, if anything of real importance was to be accomplished, to settle down upon some fixed scheme of action.

The internal improvement act of 1836 was an effort to do this. It provided for the construction, or for survey and estimates for construction, of the following: (1) The White Water canal, with connection by canal or rail with the Central canal; (2) the Central canal, along the West Fork of White river, crossing the state from northeast to southwest; (3) the extension of the Wabash and Erie canal from Tippecanoe river to Terre Haute, with connection to the Central canal; (4) a railroad from Madison to Lafayette by way of Indianapolis (5) a macadamized turnpike from New Albany to Vincennes; (6) a railroad, if practical, or a macadamized turnpike from Jeffersonville, by way of New Albany and Salem, to

Crawfordsville: (7) the removal of obstructions to the navigation of the Wabash below Vincennes; (8) a canal, or railroad, connecting the Wabash and Erie canal with Lake Michigan. This has often been called "a vast scheme," and other things indicating folly and wild disregard of reason. In reality there was nothing unreasonable about it. It provided for a total of 1,289 miles of canal, railroad and turnpike. As a matter of fact there was actually accomplished in the state within the next twenty-five years, much more in these lines than the most sanguine advocate of internal improvements had dreamed of. In 1860 there were in Indiana 2,126 miles of railroads alone. Many sneers have been leveled at the predictions of the advocates of the system that these works would be a source of profit to the state, which would relieve the people from taxation. They might not have done that, but if completed as planned they might have been as profitable as the state bank. The railroads of the state have certainly been profitable to those who built them.

The weakest point in the system, as it turned out, was the provision for canals, and yet that was the feature that had the strongest support, and was most reasonably entitled to support. Water transportation was the most important at that time from every standpoint. It was easiest and cheapest. Railroads were as yet experimental, but steamboats were assured successes. The Erie canal had been completed in 1825 and was a great success. The name of DeWitt Clinton was lauded all through the country. And there were other successful canals. The eastern division of the Pennsylvania canal, which was opened in 1830, was successful. It cost $1,737,285, and up to 1857 earned $2,333,037 net. The Delaware division of the same canal, in the same period earned about 175 per cent. on its cost. No one could foresee at that time the development of railroad transportation, and its fatal competition with the canals. And there was another fatal weakness. Our canals, like most of the others of the country, were largely built

up, as well as dug out, and were greatly exposed to danger of injury by freshets. This was not sufficiently taken into account in the estimates of maintenance and cost of construction. The Whitewater Valley canal was washed out twice before it was completed, the damage being estimated at $170,000. The small portion of the Central canal that is in use has been frequently broken at one of its built-up points by muskrats digging through the banks and starting a washout. Of course when a break in a canal occurs its business ends for some time. You cannot throw a trestle across and run slow over the break. The water is out of the entire division of the canal. This is one of the chief causes of abandonment of the high line canals in this country. In 1880 the total of abandoned canals in the United States was 1,953 miles, which cost $44,013,166, and of these there were credited to Indiana 453 miles, that cost $7,725,262. But unquestionably canals were the most feasible transportation ways in view in 1836, and everybody favored them. In fact the system adopted was a canal system with a few connecting roads where canals were not feasible. There were very few people who disapproved of the policy, but there was considerable opposition from people living in counties that did not get any roads or canals, as was most natural, and that is the reason of what opposition to the bill there was shown in the legislature. It is a sort of tradition, which has been repeated by several of our historical writers, that Gov. Whitcomb, who was in the senate in 1836, was especially opposed to the system and after its breaking down was taken up and elected governor and senator on that account. As a matter of fact Mr. Whitcomb voted for the bill.

The cause of the breaking down of the improvement plan, or at least of the distressing form it assumed, was something entirely beyond the power of the people of Indiana, something they did not anticipate, something they did not understand fully after it had occurred. The system was hardly inaugurated when the cloud appeared. The war between the federal administration and the United States bank had been on for some time, and government deposits with the bank had been stopped by the president. Under the influence of this and the strong speculative tendency in the country, large quantities of bank bills had been issued by state and private banks, and the business of the country was done chiefly in them. On July 11, 1836, under a "sound money" inspiration, the president issued a circular directing that after Aug. 15 nothing should be accepted in payment for government lands except specie or Virginia land scrip, except from actual settlers. This occasioned a vast amount of trouble and danger, for there was not specie enough available for the vast land speculating business that had grown up. Everybody was anticipating a large advance in land values, and men had contracted large liabilities on that account. When congress assembled it refused to sanction this rule, but as soon as it adjourned the president re-established it. In the meantime the withdrawal of the federal deposits from the United States bank had begun, and from these causes arose the great financial panic of 1837. It was widespread and distressing in its effects. Banks everywhere were forced to suspend specie payments, but Indiana fared better than most of the states in that her state bank currency went to a very slight discount, and the bank resumed specie payments in 1842. Prices of all kinds of property fell enormously. Bankruptcy among business men was the rule rather than the exception. The American market for securities was ruined. But hard as this blow was, Indiana could have gone on with her internal improvements, and did go on until 1839. The new source of trouble had been a supposed cause of strength. When the improvement system was under consideration the example of other states was urged in proof of its wisdom. They were all going in for improvements. They were all borrowing money, and they were all borrowing money from Europe. The drain was enormous, especially at that time, when the specie in the world was small

in amount as compared with the present. In 1830 the total debts of the states were only about $13,000,000. In 1842 the secretary of the treasury reported them at $207,894,613, with an annual interest charge of $10,394,730. The flow of gold and silver from Great Britain became alarming. In 1836 the Bank of England advanced its discount rate to 4½ per cent., and then to 5 per cent., but without avail. The drain kept on until in September, 1839, the Bank of England had but £2,406,000 in specie, and but for aid from the Bank of France would have had to suspend specie payments. It is not strange therefore that in 1839 Indiana was unable to get any money for the bonds which she had negotiated in the spring of that year. It was not that the credit of the state had failed, but that all credit had failed.

The people of Indiana made a plucky effort to save their enterprise. In 1837 Gen. Dumont appeared as an anti-improvement candidate for governor, and David Wallace as an advocate of the liberal improvement theory. In spite of panic and hard times Wallace was elected by over 9,000 majority. Both the candidates were whigs. Wallace stood staunchly by the improvements, and after the failure to raise money in 1839 issued treasury scrip to the amount of a million and a half. In 1840 the campaign had a strong flavor of national politics, though Judge Bigger, the Whig candidate, was for improvements. He defeated his opponent, Gen. Howard, by over 8,000 votes. By this time it had become evident that the state could not finish the works it had begun, and the legislature of 1841 adopted a law for turning over any of them except the Wabash and Erie canal to companies that might be organized to complete them. This was a matter of necessity, for the state could not get the money to complete them, or even meet the interest on its debt, which it was now obliged to default. The whole system had been based on the theory that the works would be paying institutions when completed, but none of them were completed, and they were not paying in their unfinished state. Obviously the best thing to be done was to get them finished at any cost, and get the advantage of opening up the country. In several cases this was done successfully. The Madison railroad was turned over in 1843 to a company which pushed it through to Indianapolis by Oct. 1, 1847. In 1849 it paid 8½ per cent. dividends on its stock. It may be mentioned in commendation of the general plan of 1836, that since then every important line of improvement then adopted has been paralleled by a railroad. The policy of turning the improvements over to private ownership was largely useful in reducing the debt, for the amount expended by the state on such works was refunded to it by the companies in state bonds, which, of course, they bought up at a discount. It was also stipulated that the works were to be completed. It was thought that the state, with government aid, could complete the Wabash and Erie canal, which had been opened from Ft. Wayne to Lafayette, and congress made another land grant in aid of it in 1841,. followed by a third, in 1845, of half the unsold lands in the Vincennes land district. The effort, however, was of no avail. The expenses were so large and the returns so small that the state could not even meet its interest payments. In 1846 Mr. Charles Butler, representing the bondholders, made a proposition to the state to take the canal, with the land grants, for half of the improvement bond debt —there had been $10,000,000 authorized and over $7,000,000 issued—with interest, if the state would issue stock bearing a low rate of interest for the remainder. The state was to have a share in the earnings over an interest equivalent, and opportunity for redemption. The canal was to be completed to Terre Haute, and the new company had the "privilege" of raising $2,500,000 and completing it to Evansville.

It was never completed, and in the course of years it became practically of no value on account of railroad competition. All of the bonds were brought in under this agreement but 191, of $1,000 each, or its equivalent in English money. Their location was unknown, and they were carried on the books of the state as part of its debt for years. In 1867 Gov. Morton called attention to this and urged that something be done to get rid of this item. Sixty-nine of these bonds were then held by the United States government as an investment for certain Indian tribes, and it had deducted the interest due on them from moneys due the state. The interest on the others had not been paid since 1841. In 1870 John W. Garrett, of Baltimore, as owner of 41 of these bonds, brought suit to foreclose them against the trustees of the Wabash and Erie canal. They were undoubtedly a lien on that canal and all the other works, and the state could not afford to allow their foreclosure, as it would have revived the entire debt disposed of by the Butler compromise. Gov. Baker laid the matter before the legislature of 1871, and it made an appropriation for their payment. At the same time he called attention to a movement then on foot to get the legislature to pay the half of the debt for which the canal had been taken, on the ground that the state had destroyed its value by granting railroad franchises. On his recommendation an amendment to the constitution was adopted preventing any assumption or payment of this claim, which was ratified by vote of the people in 1873. All of the outstanding bonds were paid under the appropriation of 1871, except twenty which did not turn up until 1877, when they were sent here for collection by their owners. The state officials refused to pay them. Another suit to foreclose was brought, and numerous parties who had become owners of parts of the old internal improvement property were made defendants. There was a hurried gathering at Indianapolis. The legislature was in session. A bill was hurried through to provide for this last remnant, and so the internal improvement debt was finally extinguished.

THE MEXICAN WAR.

The election of 1843 resulted in the defeat of Gov. Bigger by James Whitcomb, by a majority of 2,000 votes. This was the first time the Democrats had carried the state in twelve years, and the success was chiefly due to the collapse of the internal improvements under Whig management. National politics also affected the result, for the Democratic party was already taking aggressive ground in regard to Texas. In 1844 it declared for the "reannexation of Texas and the reoccupation of Oregon," and on this platform swept the country. It was almost certain that the annexation of Texas would bring war with Mexico, and in the spring of 1846 hostilities began. There was no lack of war spirit in Indiana. Eight regiments were offered, but the government called for only three, and these were promptly raised and sent to the front. The first was commanded by Col. James P. Drake; the second by Col. Jos. Lane, soon promoted to brigadier-general, who was afterwards governor and senator from Oregon; the third by Col. James H. Lane, afterwards senator from Kansas. Two other regiments were called to the field later, the fourth commanded by Col. W. A. Gorman, and the fifth by Col. Lane, formerly of the third, which had been mustered out on expiration of its term of service. In the rapid and brilliant conquest of Mexico the Indiana troops took an honorable part, but unfortunately there has been an unmerited stain left on their record through hasty criticism, and continued misrepresentation of the action of the Second Indiana regiment at the battle of Buena Vista. Briefly the facts are these: Gen. Lane, who was in command of the left wing, was informed that the enemy was advancing in force, under cover of a ravine, to turn the left flank. He sent a detachment of a part of the Second regiment and a battery of three guns, in all about 400 men, to check this movement. The enemy soon appeared, numbering about 4,000 men. The little detachment stood its ground gallantly before the approaching foe until twenty rounds had been fired. By that time a Mexican battery had gained a ridge still farther to the left, and opened a hot fire on our troops, which were as yet unsupported. At the right end of the line Gen. Lane gave the order for the battery to advance and the infantry to support it. At the left end of the line it is claimed that Col. Bowles gave the order to cease firing and retreat. The men began falling back at that end, and in a few minutes all was confusion. The elated Mexicans pressed on, but fortunately reinforcements were at hand. A Mississippi regiment reached the point first, and part of the scattered detachment rallied and continued the fight with it. The remainder gathered at the ranche in the valley where the baggage was placed, and aided in repulsing the attack at that point by the Mexican troops who had passed our line of battle. It was the opinion of dispassionate military men that the occurrence was due to the confusion of raw troops finding themselves in a critical situation, and bewildered by conflicting orders. The second Indiana regiment suffered a loss of 32 killed and 71 wounded in this battle—a loss exceeded by that of but one other regiment on the field. At the beginning of the Mexican war, there were practically no men of military training in Indiana, excepting, of course, the experience in militia drills. The experience of this war, however, was valuable, and many of the Mexican veterans rose to distinction during the civil war.

There were other matters of importance in progress in Indiana at this time besides the participation in national affairs, and one of the most memorable was the foundation of our benevolent institutions. The constitution of 1816 provided for legislation for this purpose, but nothing was done for a quarter of a century. Then agitation began for more suitable provision for the insane of the state than incarceration in county asylums, and in 1844 the legislature made provision for a tax for an insane asylum. It was located at Indianapolis, and was completed in 1847, at a cost of $75,000. The legislature of 1844 also provided for a school for the deaf and dumb, which was carried on for several years in rented quarters. The state building for this school was not completed until 1850. Agitation for provision of a school for the blind was begun but a few months later, and the legislature of 1847 made provision for a building which was completed in 1850. All of these institutions at once entered on careers of great usefulness, and though they experienced some unfortunate reverses in their early history, they have in general been liberally supported and fairly managed as to their purposes, although sometimes treated as political spoils.

Another agitation of this period was for a new state constitution, and it was well founded. The constitution of 1816 was fairly well adapted to primitive conditions, but it was now completely outgrown. Its worst defect was giving the legislature control of much business that was properly judicial, and also of much administrative business that should have been transacted by the executive department under general laws. All divorces were granted by the legislature, and the impossibility of any rational hearing of such cases by the legislature is evident. It degenerated into a farce. It is told that a bill of divorce had almost passed one legislature on the ground that the wife had given birth to a negro baby, when some one exposed the fact that both parties to the application were negroes, and the ground of action disappeared. All charters of incorporation were granted by the legislature and the legislators had become corrupt in regard to them, especially as to railroad charters, which were now becoming of importance. There was a general sentiment that every inducement should be given to private capital to carry forward the work of internal improvement at which the state had failed. The legislature also elected most of the state officers, and exercised almost unlimited power over local officers. It was no unusual thing for a legislature to abolish a county office, thereby ousting the official elected by the people, and create a new office with the same duties and elect a man to fill it. The abuses of these powers were flagrant, and their legitimate exercise required a vast amount of time. It was the ordinary thing for the local laws of a legislative session to cover four or five times as much space as the general laws. The constitutional convention assembled on October 7, 1850, and was in session for four months. Its 150 members were fairly representative of the state, and their work was very well done. Although the power of the legislature was greatly curtailed, it is probable that the gravest defect in the new constitution is still too great legislative powers. This is partly due to the decisions of the courts which have almost destroyed the inhibition of special legislation, and have left in a state of more or less uncertainty the control of the power of appointment, of districting the state for elective purposes, and of extending the terms of officials. There have been gross abuses of these powers, and in fact the great part of the controversies of state politics since then have grown out of these questions. There is a growing sentiment that all officers not elected by the people should be appointed by the executive; that their terms should not be extended by change of law; and that representation should be based on fixed political divisions, the county being the natural unit of representation. As to corporations, the new constitution and the laws under it went to the opposite extreme from the former condition. Companies were allowed to incorporate for almost any purpose without restriction, and while this served a useful purpose in developing the state, there was a looseness in the system and a lack of return to the state for privileges granted, which were not corrected until 1891 by the adoption of franchise license laws.

Another important feature of the new constitution was the provision for common schools, which was a result of a movement that had been in progress for several years. There had been a great deal of provision for "schools and seminaries of learning" in past legislation of all kinds. The ordinance of 1787, the state constitution of 1816, and numerous laws that had been passed, made excellent and liberal provision for public schools on paper, but none of them resulted in very much practically. The land grants in aid of schools were large, but the early attempts to utilize them by leasing and applying the rents to school support had not supplied revenues sufficient for more than a slight aid in meeting the expenses of tuition. There were in fact no free schools in Indiana prior to 1852, and there was no uniform general system of public instruction. There were, however, numerous schools and seminaries receiving some aid from public funds, and there were numerous private schools of more or less value. Almost every county had a seminary of some kind, corresponding in rank with our high schools, and some with our colleges, but tuition was charged in all of these. Elementary instruction was largely private, though provision was made for erecting school houses at public expense. The laws indeed declared that tuition should be free, but there were not means to make it so, and the teachers were paid by the patrons of the schools. Possibly it is a stretch of imagination to call it "pay," for the compensation received was ridiculously small, and frequently paid in supplies of various kinds. The result of this was while there was opportunity in the state for very fair education the general education of the people was neglected. By the census of 1840 Indiana stood sixteenth in the scale of illiteracy of the United States, with every other northern state, and three southern states above her. Within ten years she fell to the twenty-third place in the list, and this is not surprising, for during a part of the intervening years as high as sixty per cent. of her children of school age were not in school for one day in a year. The fact that one-seventh of the population were illiterate in 1840 roused attention, and Gov. Bigger, in his message of 1841, called attention to the practical failure of the school laws up to that time, and the unproductive nature of the school revenues. There was investigation and discussion and amendment, but nothing important was accomplished. This was due in part to the system of local legislation, on account of which there were almost as many school systems as counties, and indeed there were numerous laws applicable only to special townships.

When the legislature met in December, 1846,

there was addressed to it, through the columns of The State Journal, a communication of remarkable force and ability concerning the defects of the schools, the prevalence of illiteracy, and the necessity for a change. It began with a statement that it would discuss a topic to which neither the governor nor his predecessors had given sufficient attention, and was signed "One of the People." It, and the five succeeding similar addresses to the legislature and the constitutional convention, came to be known as the "messages" on the school question. The author was Caleb Mills, the young principal of the Presbyterian school at Crawfordsville, which afterwards became Wabash College. The legislature did not act, but the friends of public education were aroused. In May of 1847 a convention was held at Indianapolis, attended by three hundred earnest and public-spirited citizens. An address to the people was prepared, setting forth the existing evils and demanding that additional funds be provided by taxation, that the schools be made absolutely free, that they be made as good as any other schools, that a higher standard for teachers and better compensation be provided, and that a state superintendent of schools be provided. A committee was appointed to draft a law and present it to the next legislature. The next legislature did not pass any law, but it adopted a resolution submitting the question of state-supported free schools to a vote of the people at the next election. There was a great deal of division of sentiment on the question, strange as it may seem now. Some believed that parents should bear the expense of educating their children. Some regarded it as a scheme of the clergy to get control of the state. Some friends of existing schools thought it would injure them. Some thought it was an improper use of the taxing power. Some objected to diverting taxes from the locality where they were raised for any local purpose, and various other causes of objection were offered. Nevertheless, out of 140,410 votes on the question, 78,523 were for free schools and 61,887 against. Of the ninety counties then existing fifty-nine were carried for and thirty-one against. The legislature of 1849 then passed a general school law, which simplified existing regulations somewhat, levied a tax of 10 cents on $100, a poll tax of 25 cents, and a tax of 3 per cent. on insurance premiums, for the support of the schools. But the system was to apply only to such counties as voted to adopt it. At the election of 1849 fifty-nine counties voted for the law, and thirty-one against. Out of 142,-391 votes cast, 86,963 were favorable. Counties that did not accept the law in 1849 were privileged to do so thereafter, but a number of them never did so.

The fight went merrily on. Mills continued his messages to the legislature, pointing out the defects of the law and urging more radical action. Friends of the schools were active, and addresses and newspaper articles on the subject were numerous. When the constitutional convention met the subject was made prominent. It provided in the constitution for "a general and uniform system of common schools, wherein tuition should be without charge, and equally open to all." It established a common school fund as a perpetual fund that might be increased but never diminished. It provided for a state superintendent of public instruction. The principal factor of the school fund in amount, was the "sinking fund," or surplus proceeds of the state's investment in the old state bank, which was the source of over $4,255,000 of the fund. The provision for this disposition of the surplus had been included in the bank law, on motion of John Beard. From the congressional township fund—proceeds of lands reserved for school purposes—about $2,500,000 was derived. Something over $500,000 came from the surplus revenue funds divided by the United States, and over $1,000,000 has accumulated from fines and forfeitures. The other sources of the fund are small. With the constitution satisfactorily adjusted, the next thing was to get a law, and the battle for free schools was continued until the law of 1852 was passed providing for a three-months' term of absolutely free school in every district in the state. The state school tax was made 10 cents on $100, and townships were allowed to levy additional taxes to build and furnish schoolhouses, and also to continue schools after the state funds were exhausted. The latter provision was held unconstitutional by the Supreme court in 1854, as was a similar provision as to city schools two or three years later. This caused serious injury to the schools for many years, and at length in 1867 a law was enacted giving power to local taxation in aid of the schools, in defiance of these decisions. For a long time the law was not questioned, but at length a case was brought which reached the Supreme court in 1885, and it was then decided that the earlier decisions were erroneous and that the local taxes were constitutional. And well might the court so hold, for since their establishment the free schools had relieved the state of the odium of illiteracy, and brought it into the front ranks of progressive states. There has been a great deal of school legislation in later years, but nothing changing the fundamental principles of the system, though some of them have been much criticised. The school law of 1852 made the township the unit of our system and made the school township conform to the civil township. It also made the township trustee the school trustee. This was admitted to be a mistake at the time by the friends of the schools, as the same man is not apt to be a good supervisor of roads and ditches and also of schools, but the error has never been corrected. This combination of duties was largely the cause of the failure of the township libraries which were provided for by the law of 1852, and intrusted to the care of the trustees, but there were other causes still more potent, the chief of which was that there was no provision of funds for their support or increase.

From 1843 to 1861 Indiana was under Democratic control in a political way. Gov. Whitcomb was elected to succeed himself in 1846, but, being elected to the senate in 1848, his term as governor was served out by Lieut-Gov. Paris C. Dunning. In 1849 Joseph A. Wright was elected governor and re-elected in 1852 under the new constitution. He was emphatically a self-made man, and a man of much ability. He was a great champion of agriculture, and was the founder of the state board of agriculture. He attracted much notice by his active hostility to free banks and to chartering the new state bank, bills for both of which were passed over his veto. He was succeeded in 1857 by Ashbel P. Willard, one of the most brilliant orators ever known in Indiana. Gov. Willard died in 1860, and his unexpired term was filled by Lieut-Gov. Abram A. Hammond. The dominating spirit in the Democratic party at this time, however, was not one of the governors, but Jesse D. Bright, who was United States senator from 1849 to 1861. He was an adroit politician and a man of strong personal feeling, who had a love for his friends and a much stronger hatred for his enemies. During this period Indiana politics was on national lines, and the slavery question was the controlling issue. Events were rapidly hurrying the Democratic party to its great disruption, and the party in Indiana was peculiarly involved. In 1857 the Democrats had a majority of the legislature on joint ballot, but the Republicans controlled the senate and refused to meet with the house for the election of senators. The Democratic members met separately and elected Jesse D. Bright and Graham N. Fitch, who were duly commissioned. The next legislature, which was Republican, declared this election illegal, and returned Henry S. Lane and William M. McCarty. They were refused admission to the senate by a party vote, except that Stephen A. Douglas and two other Democrats voted with the Republicans to seat them. Mr. Bright never forgave this, and in the election of 1860 he organized Indiana for Breckenridge and canvassed the state for him, though the vast majoity of the Democrats, including the able younger leaders Hendricks, McDonald, Voorhees, Turpie and English supported Douglas. This removed Senator Bright from affiliation with the main wing of the party and his expulsion from the senate in 1861 for giving a letter of introduction to Thomas Lincoln, addressed to "His Excellency, Jefferson Davis, President of the Confederation of States," ended his political life. Gov. Willard, who had given evidence of becoming the popular party leader, died in 1860. Ex-Gov. Wright, who had been the strongest of the party leaders before the people, went over to the Republicans. The leadership devolved on the younger men of the party who had supported Douglas, and they took and held it.

THE CIVIL WAR.

It may be questioned whether at this time it is too early or too late to write an accurate history of the civil war—whether we have yet gained the point where an individual can see this tremendous convulsion in its true perspective, or whether we have already lost the power to appreciate the feelings of the people at that time. Fortunately that task is not imposed here, though there is much the same difficulty in presenting an account of the part Indiana took in the war. It is doubtful if even now we can enter into actual sympathy with the sentiment of 1860 in Indiana. We can see the great questions that were involved and imagine something of their effect on unbiased minds. But unbiased minds are few, and in political matters men are more often governed by the associations and prejudices of the past than by rational consideration of the problems of the present. Indiana was carried by the Republicans in 1860, but it may be questioned whether if the election had been held again three months later, the result would have been the same. The Democratic party had been dominant in Indiana, but had been losing influential members for several years on the phases of the slavery question then presented, and it had split hopelessly over the Charleston convention. The two factions were perhaps more bitter against each other than against the Republicans. The Republicans had all the lack of unanimity that characterizes a new political party. The old abolitionists voted with them, but they were not very numerous in Indiana.

The old Whigs were mostly with them, but they had repeatedly avowed that they had no hostility to slavery in its constitutional sphere. Richard W. Thompson, their most brilliant later leader in Indiana, had, in the campaign of 1855, dwelt on Whig opposition to abolitionism and his own friendship to slavery. Many Democrats voted with the Republicans in 1860, but they had no pronounced cause of hostility to their old party except the Kansas-Nebraska bill and the Dred Scott decision. Albert G. Porter, one of these, elected as a Republican to congress in 1858, and again in 1860, declared in the house of representatives his lack of sympathy for the negro, and stated that he and the Republican party in Indiana opposed the introduction of negroes in the territories on the ground that their labor should not be allowed to come in competition with white labor. The remnants of the old Knownothing organization voted with the Republicans chiefly because they were against the Democrats. The victorious Republican party of 1860 in Indiana was a strange compound of discordant elements, united through the matchless political skill of Oliver P. Morton, whose unbending will repressed extremists and forced the issues of the campaign on lines that would give offense to no element opposed to the Democratic party. It was an unusual role for Morton to play. But it was good politics and he was a prince of politicians.

After the election was over there was a noticeable revulsion of feeling. The South Carolina legislature met on Nov. 5 to cast the electoral vote of the state for Breckenridge, and it also called a convention for Dec. 19 to decide the question of secession from the Union. There was little room for doubt what that convention would do. Men were dazed by the awful alternative that was now presented of disunion or civil war, and there were undoubtedly thousands who would rather have conceded anything the south asked as to slavery in the territories than be forced to a choice between the other two. On Nov. 22 a meeting was held at Indianapolis to celebrate the Re-

publican victory. It was addressed by Henry S. Lane, the successful candidate for governor, and Oliver P. Morton, the successful candidate for lieutenant-governor, who had accepted this unimportant position on the Republican ticket, with the understanding that if it were successful Lane was to go to the senate and leave the governorship to him. Lane's speech was of the most conciliatory nature. He dwelt on the ties of friendship and commerce between Indiana and the southern states, and called to memory the generous aid that Kentucky had given in our Indian wars. Morton threw conciliation to the winds. The great question before the people was the coercion of South Carolina if she attempted secession, and that was no question to him. Coercion was simply enforcement of the law. There was no power in a state to secede and no power in a president to permit it. We must either admit the independence of South Carolina or compel its submission. The former meant the disruption of the Union, and, aside from other considerations, this would be intolerable to the inland states because they would be shut off from communication with the seaboard except through independent nations. Even if the effort to coerce South Carolina should fail it were better that it fail after an appeal to arms, for that at least would be notice that no other state should go except after a like struggle. There would be no encouragement to secession in that course. "If it was worth a bloody struggle to establish this nation, it is worth one to preserve it; and I trust that we shall not, by surrendering with indecent haste, publish to the world that the inheritance which our fathers purchased with their blood we have given up to save ours. Seven years is but a day in the life of a nation, and I would rather come out of a struggle at the end of that time defeated in arms and conceding independence to successful revolution, than purchase present peace by the concession of a principle that must inevitably explode this nation into small and dishonored fragments." This was very radical sentiment for that day, and it is fairly beyond question that it was not the sentiment of a majority of the people of Indiana. Yet the logic of the speech was perfect, and the end was inevitable. The people simply were not prepared for it. There were other men who saw it, but few who ventured to say so. Doubtless Mr. Lincoln saw it as clearly, but fortunately for the country he realized that the people did not yet comprehend the full meaning of the situation, and that the attitude, not only of the border states, but of some of the western states, would depend on the movement of events. They wanted the Union preserved, but to make it evident that the Union was threatened the south must be put plainly in the attitude of aggression. He said to the southern states in his inaugural: "The government will not assail you. You can have no conflict without being yourselves the aggressors. You have no oath registered in heaven to destroy the government, while I shall have the most solemn one to preserve, protect and defend it." It was undoubtedly due to the wise policy of Mr. Lincoln that when the attack on Fort Sumter came it was almost universally recognized as an act of treason, and the people understood thoroughly that the issue was the preservation of the Union.

From that time there was a notable change. Indecision disappeared. There was general agreement that the authority of the national government must be maintained. Mr. Douglas took strong ground for the support of the administration in the prosecution of the war. Mr. Hendricks and other Indiana Douglas leaders were equally explicit in their declarations. There was a great awakening of the war spirit. When Mr. Lincoln issued his call for 75,000 volunteers on April 15, the response was immediate. Indiana's quota was 4,683 men. Within a week after the call twelve thousand volunteers were at Camp Morton eager to be sent to the front. On the 19th Gov. Morton called the legislature to meet in special session on the 24th. He sent in a vigorous war message and asked the appropriation of $1,-000,000 for war purposes. The legislature was responsive. Its appropriations reached twice

that amount. The militia law was revised to meet the emergency. Provision was made for enlisting troops in excess of the government's call. Every provision suggested was adopted for putting the state on a war footing. The same legislature at its regular session in January had shown a strong desire to conciliate the south and avoid war. At the special session but one member suggested anything that could be considered conciliatory, and his resolutions were unanimously rejected. Meanwhile the executive department was moving with tremendous energy. The legislature had scarcely met when the first brigade of Indiana troops was sent to the front. It was hurried through Cincinnati to West Virginia and took a leading part in the first regular campaign of the war which destroyed secession in that region and made the actual division of Virginia which soon became a legal reality. Morton was a "war governor" in the fullest sense of the word. He not only supplied troops in advance of calls, but armed and equipped them and insisted on the government's taking them. Nor were his communications to the administration limited to this. He bombarded Lincoln and Stanton with letters insisting on greater energy and more pronounced measures. He demanded the appointment of generals who would do something. He suggested plans for campaigns in the Mississippi valley and offered to go in person to conduct them. He kept them informed on all movements discovered by his vigilant emissaries that could give aid or comfort to the enemy. Unquestionably it was due to his relentless energy that Indiana made the great record she did in supporting the prosecution of the war. The state furnished a total of 196,363 men in the war, and 784 paid money commutation for exemption from service. On this basis Indiana furnished 74.3 per cent of her total population capable of bearing arms, according to the census of 1860, to the armies of the Union. On this basis but one state in the Union surpassed or equalled her record and that was Delaware, which is credited with 74.8 per cent. of her military population of

1860. But of the supply credited to Delaware one-tenth was in money commutation, and nearly one-tenth of the men were colored. On an estimate (Fox's Regimental Losses) made on the basis of white troops actually furnished for three years of service, Indiana supplied 57 per cent. of her military population of 1860— i. e., the males between 18 and 45 years of age. On this basis she was surpassed by only one state, Kansas, whose record was 59.4 per cent. But Kansas furnished in the aggregate less than one-tenth the troops Indiana furnished, and the frontier conditions existing then made it less onerous for a large proportion of fighting men to go to the front. Of the troops sent by Indiana 7,243 were killed or mortally wounded on the battlefield, and 19,429 died from other causes, making a total death loss of over 13 per cent. of all troops furnished.

Moreover, Indiana acted as a sort of protector to the border. The first call came from Kentucky for protection from one of John Morgan's raids, and the next from Cincinnati, which had probably fallen into the hands of Kirby Smith but for the prompt appearance of aid from Indiana. Three times, indeed, Indiana was invaded. The first was at Newburg, in Warrick county, in 1862, by a small party from Kentucky, who seemed more bent on plunder than on war, and who escaped across the river before any active resistance could be made. In June, 1863, a small body of confederate cavalry under Capt. Thos. H. Hines, crossed the Ohio near Cannelton, and did some plundering, but they were run down and captured. In July of the same year came the Morgan raid, which was the most important that occurred. Morgan had been sent out by Gen. Bragg to make a raid through Kentucky, but violated his orders and crossed the Ohio at Brandenburg with nearly 2,500 men. He advanced rapidly through the southern part of the state, looting stores and levying ransoms on mill-owners and others to save their property from destruction. Horses of any value were taken wherever found. But Morgan soon saw that he had made a mistake in coming into

Indiana. The idea that there was a large sentiment here favorable to secession and that the people would rise against the government if invasion gave them opportunity was quickly dispelled. There were practically no troops in the state, and Gov. Morton called for volunteers. Within a few hours thousands were on their way to Indianapolis, and within two days 20,000 had been enlisted at that point, while twice that number were organized and prepared for service elsewhere. Wherever Morgan went he found militia preparing to meet him. Some small forces he captured, but from others he turned away and pursued his course, seeking to get back across the Ohio. But orders had gone out to watch all available points for crossing and keep boats out of reach. The militia were now concentrating all along the river and pushing after the raiders. Morgan made his way out of Indiana and into Ohio, striking the river at the shoals of Buffington island, where he had hoped to ford, but the river was high and impassable. At this point part of his force was captured. Morgan with a few hundred escaped and most of them were captured after they had almost reached the Pennsylvania line. The raid really had a valuable effect for it not only impressed on the Democrats that they were confronting war in which their homes might need protection, but also showed the Republicans that Democratic neighbors whom, in the heat of political strife, they had suspected of treasonable sentiments, were in fact loyal to the flag and ready to rally to its defense in case of need.

It was a beneficial thing that this manifestation of a common loyalty came when it did, for there had grown up not a little bitter feeling over political matters. Everybody concedes that in time of war it is the duty of the loyal citizen to give his support to his country against the enemy, but at the same time it is not desirable in a free country that political differences should be dropped. In time of war there is naturally a tendency to undue exercise of power on the part of the administration, and it is important that a conservative organization should be in existence for purposes of restraint. On the other hand it is frequently necessary to resort to extremes in time of war. The old maxim was that "in time of war the laws are silent." The important thing is that the laws be not overridden without necessity, and there will frequently arise questions as to that. The civil war was prolific of such questions. It was begun to save the Union and the constitution, and it is doubtful if the people of the north would have gone into it on any other basis. And yet it was soon found that the constitution must be made very elastic. One of the first questions was the admission of West Virginia. Could a sovereign state be divided, without even its consent and a new state created? Some defended the constitutionality of the step, but Thaddeus Stevens boldly said he would not stultify himself by pretending it was constitutional. It was a necessity of war, and he favored it. Then came the never-ending negro question. The proposal to emancipate the slaves and utilize them in subduing the south was widely agitated in 1862. It was urged as a war measure. It was opposed as unconstitutional and dangerous. It might lead to servile insurrection in the south, and it meant a revolution to the north. If you put the musket in the negro's hand you must consistently follow it with the ballot. This had a wide effect in 1862. The people had not gone to war to free the negro. Moreover the progress of the war had been very unsatisfactory. With the exception of Grant's victories in the west there was little to inspire hope of success in bringing the southern states under federal control. The presence of troops throughout the northern states and the zeal of some of the officials led to encroachments on individual rights. Numerous military arrests were made on ground of suspicion of treasonable conduct, but these arrests, which were quite numerous in Indiana, were productive of so much criticism that the presidential order under which they were made was revoked in November, 1862.

These various causes produced a revulsion of feeling in Indiana in 1862, and the state and legislative elections were carried by the Democrats. The legislature met with a feeling on the part of Democrats that civil liberty was being needlessly encroached upon, and that the executive power should be restrained to constitutional limits. On the other hand the Republican or Union members as they were then called, felt that the safety of the country lay in the possession of full power by an executive devoted to the preservation of the Union at any cost, even if civil liberty suffered somewhat. The result was a practical deadlock. The Republican members bolted in a body, and went to Madison to prevent legislation. The Democrats refused to make any appropriations, expecting to force a special session. This affected only the state government. The legislature had made elections to the national senate, Thomas A. Hendricks for the full term, and David Turpie for the unexpired term of Jesse D. Bright, who had been expelled from the senate, which was being filled temporarily by ex-Gov. Wright, by appointment. But no special session was called. Gov. Morton assumed the responsibility of conducting the state government without appropriations, and until the close of the war the administration of affairs was more nearly on a military basis than at any time since Major Hamtramck turned this region over to the civil authorities. The situation is aptly expressed by Mr. Foulke, Gov. Morton's biographer, who puts his account of this period under the title, "I am the state." The governor borrowed money to conduct the state institutions and to do whatever he thought necessary in the prosecution of the war. Indeed, he had done this before, for on account of the difficulty of getting arms and equipment with satisfactory speed he had established an arsenal and manufactured what was wanted, at times supplying neighboring states or the federal government in emergencies. His transactions in these lines amounted to millions of dollars, but they were conducted honestly and the state did not suffer from them. A few of the officials appointed by him were not so scrupulous in their dealings, but they were removed when their shortcomings were discovered. As has been said, the Morgan raid reconciled the people to this state of affairs, and also produced a much better feeling among the enthusiastic war men, who saw that their neighbors were not so lacking in loyalty as they had imagined.

The experience also enabled the people to receive with some appreciation of their true significance the exposures of the "Knights of the Golden Circle," and the "Sons of Liberty" a little later. There were secret organizations formed in Indiana during the war, and with the natural result that in some regions there was more or less lawlessness on both sides, somewhat similar to the later whitecapping experiences. The original organization among Democrats was begun on the plea of necessity of protection from lawless neighbors, and an attempt was made to make it general. Prominent Democratic leaders were invited to join it, but the more intelligent not only declined to do so, but warned the others that they could enter upon no folly more stupendous; that even if their purposes were proper the inevitable tendency in time of war in such an organization would be to drift toward something treasonable; that whatever care they might take in their organization it would soon be filled with detectives and spies, and their political enemies would be in possession of all their secrets. The warnings were of avail as to the great mass of the party but there were a few men of some influence who joined them and carried a more ignorant following with them. It was at the close of a period when secret organization had been carried to extreme lengths and mystic ceremonies and hair-raising obligations had become so common that the country had been well prepared for that gigantic burlesque, "The Sons of Malta," which had taken the nation by storm. There were, however, many remaining to whom the experience of mystery and secret organization was almost a necessity of existence. As is commonly the case in such organizations there arose "circles within circles," and this progressed until the real "secrets of the order" were in the hands of a very few of the members, though they were known all the time to outsiders. It is not probable that there were twenty thousand men in Indiana in any of these organizations, and the majority of these never had any idea that anything treasonable was intended. Many had joined and after going through the initiatory stage had dropped out of any active participation in the meetings or proceedings of the order, and, like many who remained in, were never informed on the ulterior purposes of the leaders. Moreover, there was within the outer organization a military department or degree, independent of the "civil order," and to which a large number of the nominal members did not belong, though the leaders of the order were members of both. The ritual was fantastic to the border of the ridiculous, and may well serve as an index to the character of the members to whom the organization was, in fact, a serious thing. That there were such men is unquestionable, and that in some way they impressed on the minds of the confederate authorities that they represented a formidable following is probably true. But it is not credible that a tenth of even the nominal membership of the orders would have followed the leaders in their insane projects. Any attempt to inaugurate an insurrection in the north would have proven as pronounced a failure as the uprising that was to have occurred at the time of Morgan's raid.

Moreover, the idea that there was ever any real danger from these organizations is unfounded. The statement of Gov. Morton's biographer may be accepted without hesitancy that, "No one can read the history of the secret organizations in Indiana and not feel that, widespread as they were, there was not an instant in which they were not securely within the grasp of the war governor." He had members in all of their lodges, and received daily reports of all proceedings. There is no question of this. His biographer naively says: "It was ostensibly by others that they were exposed and overthrown, but many of the secret agents employed were his emissaries, and those who have examined the reports made to him at each step in the plot can understand how completely these organizations were under his control, how he played with them as a cat with a mouse, how he even permitted them to grow and develop that he might fasten conviction more securely upon them and overthrow them utterly when the time should be ripe for their destruction." Indeed, the detectives and agents of Morton were so numerous and influential as to give color to the charge that he directed the movements of the order. Whenever one of them became suspected by his associate members he was at once arrested by the military, loaded with irons, and treated with such indignity that when released he stood as a martyr and received the fullest confidence of the conspirators. The military part of this detective work was in charge of Gen. H.B. Carrington, a man well fitted by nature for that sort of work, though utterly unfitted for military command, as was demonstrated in 1866, when the Sioux massacred his troops at Ft. Phil Kearney and forced his abandonment of the Powder river country. One of the detectives operating under Carrington in Indiana and Kentucky, Felix Stidger by name, was so active in the cause that he was made grand secretary of Kentucky. In brief, there is no room to question the statement of Morton's biographer, "So complete was this system of espionage that Morton and Carrington often knew the most important plans of the order before they were communicated to the members who were expected to take part in their execution." And there is no reason to doubt that this intimate knowledge of the designs of the order was used for political purposes. Gov. Morton regarded the safety of the Union as dependent on the supremacy of the Republican party, and he used his power to secure that result in elections as freely as he did in the administration of the state government. He not only permitted these organizations "to grow and develop," but he arranged that the "time should be ripe" for

exposure in the middle of the political campaign of 1864. At the "indignation meeting" held at Indianapolis on August 22 of that year, after the exposure of the "Sons of Liberty," Gov. Morton, after detailing the affairs of the order with plentiful suggestions of political bearing, said: "It is all one thing to Jefferson Davis whether we fail by means of a defeat at the coming elections or by the overthrow of Union arms in the field." On Oct. 8, Carrington issued a manifesto on the exposure, closing with the words: "You can rebuke this treason. The traitors intend to bring war to your homes. Meet them at the ballot box while Grant and Sherman meet them in the field." These expressions are merely samples of many showing that politics was never out of mind in connection with this matter. Indeed, throughout the campaign a military court which had been instituted in September, was in session trying the ringleaders of the organization, and sentenced part of them to death and others to imprisonment. That it was utterly illegal cannot be questioned because the case was taken before the Supreme court on writ of habeas corpus, and it so decided. The courts were open in Indiana, but they could not be handled so promptly for display purposes. Gov. Morton either knew that this proceeding was illegal all the time, or very early became convinced of it, for he went to a great deal of trouble to prevent the execution of the convicted prisoners after Andrew Johnson had become president, and was fired with a zeal to "make treason odious," greater than his knowledge of the case. Gov. Morton was not inhuman. After he had accomplished his purpose he had no desire to push his wretched dupes to death, at least by illegal methods.

It is perhaps hardly worth while to complain of unfairness in politics, but there was one thing in connection with all this conspiracy business that left a lasting impression on the minds of some people and that was very unjust. It was the effort to throw suspicion of treason on some of the Democratic leaders—notably Mr. Voorhees and Mr. Hendricks—and this effort is continued by misguided partisans to this day. Both of these gentlemen were candidates for office on the Democratic ticket, and both were disliked personally by Morton. For these reasons no effort was spared to smirch their characters as to their loyalty. It even went so far as a seizure of papers alleged to belong to Voorhees by Gen. Carrington, in an office that had not been occupied by him for some months, he being in congress at the time. It is not necessary to go into the details of the case, as it may be disposed of on general considerations. In the first place Morton unquestionably knew exactly who the members of the secret organizations were, and watched them for months with special regard to political effects. He never hesitated to call by name any man in any way connected with the order or to say that he was a member, but never at any time did he state that Voorhees was a member. Secondly, nobody ever questioned the exact loyalty of Joseph E. McDonald at any time, and throughout this whole period he and Mr. Hendricks and Mr. Voorhees were on terms of the closest intimacy and friendship. The truth is that the secret organizations were a thorn in the flesh of the Democratic leaders which they had made unavailing efforts to get rid of. When it was finally learned that the leaders of the Sons of Liberty actually intended open treason, it was at once decided that the government should be notified and the movement stopped. But Mr. McDonald, who performed this duty, was coolly informed by Gov. Morton that he knew all about the treasonable proposals and had his spies all through the order. The "exposure" was sprung soon after, and the Democratic leaders who had given warning found themselves charged at least with encouraging the conspiracy. Such is politics. But a vast injustice has been done by it to both Mr. Hendricks and Mr. Voorhees, and doubtless it will continue to stain their memories, in the minds of ignorant and bigoted partisans. And there was another thing done in this connection that was utterly unjustifiable. Among the letters seized by Carrington were a number of a private character, having no reference in any particular to any treason charges, but having political bearing in other ways. These were retained and published for purely political purposes with full knowledge that they were stolen property.

The Republicans carried the state in 1864—by great frauds it was charged, and with some intimidation it is conceded, and this was the last campaign of the war. The close came in 1865, and it was welcomed by all, for the country was tired indeed of the long and bloody struggle. In it Indiana had borne a proud part. Not only had she stood at the front in furnishing troops, but the troops she had furnished had stood among the foremost in their fighting. The burdens of the people had been heavy. Besides the state expenditures and the heavy national taxes, the counties had expended over $20,000,000 for bounties and relief to the soldiers and their families. It was a day of pride and gladness when the victorious troops came home. It was a triumph of the Union and also of Indiana. Gen. Lew Wallace expressed the state's claims well at the time in these words: "I will not say that Indiana's contributions to the cause were indispensable to final success. That would be unjust to states more populous and wealthy, and equally devoted. But I will say that her quotas precipitated the result; without them the war might yet be in full progress and doubtful. Let us consider this proposition a moment. At Shiloh Indiana had thirteen regiments; at Vicksburg she had twenty-four; at Stone River twenty-five; at Chickamauga twenty-seven; at Mission Ridge twenty; in the advance from Chattanooga to Atlanta fifty; at Atlanta Sherman divided them so that exactly twenty-five went with him down to the sea, while twenty-five marched back with Thomas and were in at the annihilation of Hood at Nashville. What a record is thus presented. Ask Grant, or Rosecrans, or Sherman, if from the beginning to the end of their operations there was a day for which they could have spared those regiments."

There was not a great deal of political feeling in the legislature of 1865, and the constitutional amendment abolishing slavery was passed with little show of opposition. It was a relief to everybody to have it gone, and, indeed, nine-tenths of the Indiana Democrats had been opposed to it, at least so far as its extension was concerned, before the war began. Everybody was glad to return to the pursuits of peace and conditions were favorable to great industrial progress. To many men the war experience had been a liberal education. The soldier had much to do beside fighting. There were roads to make, bridges to build, railroad and telegraph lines to replace during the great contest, and there were few soldiers who did not return with increased ability to do anything that came to hand. Indeed whole Indiana regiments had been transferred to the engineer department at various times. People turned their attention to making money, and politics almost dropped out of sight. Just after the legislative session of 1865 Gov. Morton suffered a paralytic stroke and went to France for treatment, leaving Lieut.-Gov. Baker in charge. On his return in 1866 he opened the campaign with one of the bitterest speeches ever heard in Indiana, and from that time forward the war was fought over for political purposes for the next ten years. The Republicans were successful in the election, and the legislature returned Gov. Morton to the senate. In 1868 there was another bitter campaign, acting governor Baker and Thomas A. Hendricks being the candidates for governor. The official returns showed a majority of 961 for Baker, but the Democrats claimed that this was obtained by manipulation of the returns, though no contest was made. The issues had been largely the reconstruction of the southern states and negro suffrage. The legislature was Republican in both branches, but there were not enough Republican members to make a quorum. When the question of ratifying the 15th amendment was pressed on the legislature the Democratic members all resigned. Gov.

Baker issued writs for elections to fill the vacancies and called a special session for April 8. When this assembled the same question was again presented, and the Democratic members again handed their resignations to the governor. This time Morton was on hand and in command. The resignations were not reported to the two houses, and the next day when the Democratic members returned for their effects the doors of the senate were locked and Lieut.-Gov. Isaac P. Gray counted the Democratic senators as present and not voting. The Democratic representatives escaped, but the speaker ruled that a quorum of the members was present, and so Indiana was counted for the amendment. The Democrats carried the next legislature and attempted to rescind the action of its predecessor, but the Republican members prevented it by resigning in a body.

The election of 1872 was peculiar. Mr. Greeley had been indorsed by the Democrats for the presidency, and the Indiana Democrats had again nominated Mr. Hendricks for governor. The former was as unpopular with Democrats as the latter was popular. At the state election in October Mr. Hendricks defeated his opponent, Gen. Thomas M. Browne, by 1,148 votes, the only other successful candidate on the Democratic ticket being Milton B. Hopkins, for superintendent of public instruction. In November the state was carried by Grant by a majority of 22,924. Mr. Hendricks was the first Democratic governor elected in a northern state after the war. The legislature of 1873 was distinguished by the passage of the Baxter bill, a very radical liquor law, and this was the cause of the political reversal in the elections of 1874, which were carried by the Democrats by 18,000 plurality. The legislature of 1875 repealed the law. The campaign of 1876 was an interesting one in Indiana. The platform of "reform" was inspiring to many who had become weary of carpet-bag government in the south. Mr. Hendricks was on the national ticket as a candidate for vice-president. For governor the Democratic candidate was James D. Williams, familiarly known as "Blue Jeans." The Republicans nominated for this office Godlove S. Orth, but during the campaign, on account of charges of connection with certain Venezuela claims, he withdrew from the ticket, and Gen. Benj. Harrison, a clean and strong man, was put in his place. The election resulted favorably for the Democrats, the majority for Gov. Williams being 5,184. The Democrats elected their state ticket and a majority of the state senate, but lost the house on account of the apportionment law of 1872. This division in the legislature led to provision for building a new state house, for which neither political party wished to assume full responsibility. In 1880 the pendulum swung back and the Republicans carried the state for Garfield by 6,641. At the same time Albert G. Porter was elected governor. The legislature was Republican, and elected Gen. Harrison to the senate. This legislature also proposed an amendment to the constitution providing for a prohibitory liquor law. This caused a revulsion of political sentiment, and the legislature of 1883 was carried by the Democrats. It made provision for the erection of three new insane asylums, at Richmond, Logansport and Evansville. In 1884 the Democratic ascendency continued, the plurality for Mr. Cleveland being 6,512. In 1888 the state changed again giving 2,348 plurality for Harrison. In 1892 Harrison lost the state to his former opponent by 7,125. In 1896 Indiana swung back into the Republican column with a plurality of 18,181 for McKinley. From 1872 no political party carried Indiana in two successive presidential elections.

There were of course numerous causes that contributed to this result, but it is probable that "hard times" has had a good deal to do with it. It has often been said that "no political party could survive a panic," and there is usually confirmation for it. Many people instinctively blame the party in power if they are not successful in business, and give it credit if they are prosperous, without any especial consideration of what it has done or has not done. It is

a disposition to try some change. The panic of 1873 was severely felt in Indiana. The state had great natural resources, and, as has been mentioned, the men who returned from the war were much better acquainted with the methods of work on large scales than when they went in. There had also been a departure from the slow and conservative business processes of peace. A spirit of adventure and enterprise had been developed. The natural resources of the state furnished fields for legitimate use of much of it. Population was increasing rapidly. Railroads were being built. Real estate was advancing in value. But counteracting all these was a silent force. During the war the country had come to a paper money basis, and the prices and business of the country had become adjusted to that basis. The paper was largely depreciated. After the war it began to appreciate, simply from the improved credit of the government, and by that force alone came to within about ten per cent. of specie value. Nobody realized the meaning of the change, or of the effect it had on all contracts. If a man agrees to deliver so many acres of land, or so many bushels of wheat, he understands readily that a change in the size of an acre or of a bushel changes his undertaking, but at that time nobody realized that a dollar was a measure and that its value was changing. And in fact it did change but little practically until 1873, for the other forces mentioned counteracted its effect, and prices were held up, nominally at least, until the crash was precipitated by a money stringency in Europe. Then the whole force of the change came in one blow, and it was a terrific blow. Nevertheless there was power of resistance, for the natural wealth of the state was great and the people did not succumb without a struggle. The first move was to avoid the pressure by borrowing money and money was borrowed freely. By corrected returns the private mortgage debt of the state increased from June 1, 1872, to June 1, 1879, over $60,000,000. But this does not show the full extent of this movement, because before 1879 many men had seen their property swallowed up for debt, and their mortgages had been "satisfied" by foreclosure and sale, and therefore do not appear in this statement of increasing volume of secured debt. The foreclosures of mortgages in the federal courts for Indiana by thirteen foreign insurance companies alone, for the year 1878, amounted to $703.971.80, and this fact does not give an exaggerated idea of the extent to which debt was being cancelled by the transfer of property at that time. The property went at a ruinously low vaulation, for the large amount forced on the market put it far below normal valuation even when the change in the money standard was allowed for. And the change in the actual standard had been going on all the time, for in 1874 the resumption of specie payments had been directed to be made on Jan. 1, 1879, and the actual measure of value in use by the whole country continued to appreciate to that time. Of course most men did not understand the significance of the change. Many accepted readily the theory that their troubles were due to the fact of the use of depreciated paper, and were anxious to get back to a specie basis. Others remembered only that there had been "good times" under the paper basis, and desired to remain with a permanent greenback currency, to be inflated whenever the country "needed" it, which would mean whenever there were "hard times." But so long as times were hard there were always enough to follow the theory of putting out the party in power, without any material consideration of anything else. And times continued hard. The bankruptcies in Indiana ran at the average of about one hundred a year at the beginning of the '70s, gradually increasing to 294 in 1876, 405 in 1877, and 835 in the first eight months of 1878. The bankruptcy law went out by repeal on Aug. 31, 1878, and this of course led many to give up the struggle and begin over. No one who did not live in Indiana and know the actual reverses of families that supposed themselves wealthy, can fully realize the revolutionary character of this great depression or of the ef-

fect it probably had on the views of the people. After 1878 there was a breathing spell, and an improvement in conditions. Prices regained something like a normal plane. But in 1884 came another panic and industrial depression. In 1890 came another. In 1893 came a still greater. Fortunately the state was aided in resisting the effects of these collapses by vast discoveries of oil and natural gas which not only added directly to natural production but caused the location of manufactories and a large influx of population. Money has poured into the state from the outside seeking investment, and it is only to be regretted that so much of it will cause a withdrawal of profits to foreign investors to be expended elsewhere. The people have never yet realized the full meaning of non-resident ownership, and the advantage of having the profits of business expended where they are made.

There was another movement in Indiana in this period that was due in part at least to "hard times." It has been noted by historians that reforms spring from discontent. People who are satisfied have no desire for change. But just as a bodily pain causes the individual to seek for medicinal relief, a distress in the body politic causes people to seek for a remedy. And when one faction assigns one cause for the troubles and prescribes a remedy, another naturally seeks for some other cause. In this way the whole field is looked over and there are usually found various points at which improvements can be made. That is why reforms come in cycles. Such was the result that prominently manifested itself in Indiana in the legislature of 1889. The Republicans had carried the nation and the state, but the Democrats controlled the legislature. They claimed that they had been defeated in Indiana by fraud in the elections, and showed their sincerity by causing a large number of arrests to be made. They went further in the legislature and adopted the Australian ballot law in its most stringent form, including some provisions for the purity of the ballot not elsewhere known. They also adopted very stringent anti-bribery laws, the most important and most effective of which was recently repealed by the legislature of 1899. Another important measure adopted in 1889 was a school book law, designed to reduce the expense of public education by destroying monopoly in school books and frequent changes of books in use. It has succeeded admirably in these regards, and has reduced the expense for books of patrons of the schools over fifty per cent. Another very important law, designed to correct abuses which had been manifested at various times in the management of penal and charitable institutions, was one establishing a board of state charities, having a general power of supervision and investigation over all public institutions of this character but with no power of interference except by making public anything objectionable discovered. Another law aimed to relieve the pressure of the burden of public improvements by providing a system of bond issues for such expense, and payment in ten annual installments. This system has given a great impetus to public improvements, and is in part the cause of the great change in appearance of many Indiana towns and cities. In the legislature of 1891 the effort to relieve the burdens of the tax payer resulted in the revision and improvement of the tax law, which was intended to make corporations bear a more just proportion of public burdens, and which has had that result to a large extent. This law has been used as a model in several other states, as have some of the others mentioned. Another law passed at this session, after vigorous opposition, was a fee and salary law, putting state and county officials on salaries, and requiring the fees collected by them to be paid into the public treasuries. Owing to legal defects this law had to be re-enacted by subsequent legislatures before it became fully enforcible. A great forward step in municipal reform was taken by this legislature in the adoption of a new city charter for Indianapolis, which is generally recognized as model for city government. It has been followed in its general lines in charters for other cities by subsequent legislatures.

There have also been some minor reform measures adopted since 1891, and of them the ones of the most radical character are those for the reform of county and township government adopted in 1899. The most important feature of these laws is the introduction of a legislative body in such governments, and a separation of legislative and executive functions. These laws have not yet been tried, but it is believed by their advocates that they will have very beneficial results. Also worthy of mention are a compulsory education law passed in 1897, and an insurance law passed in 1899. The latter removes an absurd provision which for years has prevented the formation of home companies, and it will doubtless result in the establishment of sound companies in Indiana which will prevent the drain of money from the state for insurance.

Indiana has steadily increased in population and aggregate wealth. In 1860 the total population was 1,350,428; in 1870 it was 1,680,637; in 1880 it was 1,978,301; in 1890 it was 2,192,404. Of this total at the last census, 45,668 were colored, and 146,205 were of foreign birth. Of the foreign born 84,900 were from Germany and 35,855 from Great Britain. The majority of the people of Indiana have always been engaged in agriculture, though the proportion has been steadily decreasing. In 1890 of 635,080 persons engaged in occupations there were 331,240 engaged in agriculture, but the manufactures have grown materially since then, and it is probable that agriculture will not have a clear majority at the next census. The returns of assessed valuation show a more rapid growth in property than in population. In 1860 the total assessed value of all property in the state was $411,042,424; in 1870 it was $663,455,044; in 1880 it was $727,815,131; in 1890 it was $856,838,472; in 1898 it was $1,285,965,056. The great change in the last eight years is chiefly due to a change in the system of valuation under the tax law of 1891, as the assessed value was put up to $1,255,256,038 in 1891. However, the actual wealth of the state has increased more than is indicated by a comparison of the figures for 1891 and 1898, which really indicate a slipping back toward the old evil of extreme undervaluation. In 1890 the national authorities estimated the true valuation of the state at $2,095,176,626. Railroad mileage has increased steadily from 3,177 miles in 1870 to 4,373 miles in 1880, then to 6,109 miles in 1890; then to 6,598 miles in 1898. This includes 305 miles of "second main," or double track. The development of manufactures presents a notable movement in labor conditions. In 1860 the number of manufacturing establishments was 5,323 and the number of employes 21,295. In 1870 there were 11,847 establishments and 58,852 employes. In 1880 there were only 11,198 establishments, but 69,-508 employes. In 1890 there were 12,354 establishments and 124,349 employes. In other words, in 1860 the average was 4 employes to the establishment; in 1870 nearly 5; in 1880 more than 6; and in 1890 more than 10. The significance of this is that the independent artisan who had his little shop is largely disappearing before the advance of large concerns with their advantages of capital and machinery. The discovery and use of natural gas has made a large increase in the manufacturing of the state since 1890. The flow of this fuel is estimated at over 900,000,000 cubic feet per day, and its value at over $5,000,000 per year. The oil product of the state is about 5,000,000 barrels per year, and the coal product between 4,000,000 and 5,000,000 tons per year.

At the close of the term of Gov. Albert G. Porter in 1885, he was succeeded in office by Isaac Pusey Gray, who served until 1889, and was succeeded by Alvin P. Hovey. Gov. Hovey died in office in 1891, and was succeeded by Lieut.-Gov. Ira J. Chase, who served the remainder of the term. He was succeeded in 1893 by Claude Matthews, who served a full term of four years. The present governor, James A. Mount, then came into office. During his term the Cuban war came on, and Indiana displayed an eager patriotism in the national movement to aid the Cubans. Volunteers offered far in excess of the calls for troops, and there was intense rivalry in securing the opportunity to go to the front. But the desire of the soldiers for actual service was largely disappointed. The 27th battery reached Porto Rico, and was just going into action beyond Guayama when a messenger brought news of the signing of the peace protocol, and hostilities were stopped. The 161st infantry was sent to Cuba after the war was over, leaving Savannah in December, 1898. The other regiments were not allowed to see foreign soil, but some of them underwent severe experiences in southern camps. The hardships of the 157th regiment at Fernandina, Fla., were especially serious, and the losses by sickness while in service are said to have been exceeded by deaths among the men since they were mustered out, from diseases contracted in service. The number of troops furnished by Indiana in this war was 7,301. Of course the state had numerous representatives in the regular army and in the navy, all of whom served with credit, and reflected honor on their state.

A BASIS FOR STATE PRIDE.

There has been a great deal said at one time and another about the great natural resources of Indiana, her coal fields, her great supplies of oil and natural gas, her wonderful quarries of building stone, her clays and her fertile soil, so much indeed that one might well wonder whether we have a climate and soil to produce great men. It is believed by some ethnologists that the human race is affected by its material surroundings, and though the thought may be fanciful, it is one that is attractive. It is easy to enter into the spirit of the impassioned Wendell Phillips in his eloquent tribute to the American Indian and the brave stand he made for his native land through centuries of warfare against the hordes the world poured out upon him—a record which neither Greek, nor Scot, nor Kelt, nor Briton can equal. "I love the American Indian, for I believe that there is something in the climate and soil that moulded him that is destined in the centuries to come to mould us." If this theory be well founded, this section of the country need have nothing to fear, for among the list of distinguished natives, none hold prouder places than Pontiac, Tecumseh and Little Turtle—men of breadth, of enlightenment, of native power rarely surpassed in the record of uncivilized races. But most men will take a more practical view of human development, and ascribe the production of great men to the civilization of the community that begets them. They assume that there must be some foundation, some food for growth. They do not believe that great men spring like mushrooms in the dark without any apparent cause. There must be favorable conditions for growth.

Indiana is a young state. She is barely completing the first century of organized government, and yet Indiana's product of distinguished men is one that will bear comparison with that of other states. When we speak of distinguished men in this country we turn naturally to men in public life. What has Indiana done? She has furnished to the nation one president, two vice-presidents, three speakers of the house of representatives, a secretary of war, two secretaries of state, two secretaries of the treasury, two secretaries of the interior, a secretary of the navy, two postmasters-general and one attorney-general. Nor has the record been one of office-holding merely. Morton and Hendricks, Harrison and McDonald, Colfax and Kerr, McCulloch and Gresham are names that will be preserved while the history of the nation lasts, as of men whose services entitled them to the memory of their fellowmen. And Indiana has furnished statesmen to her sister states. Of governors may be mentioned Harding of Utah; Blaisdell of Nevada; Lane of Oregon; Burnside of Rhode Island, and there were probably a score more of them, while the list of judges, senators, representatives and other high officials will run up into the hundreds. In each of our recent congresses there sat almost as many men of Indiana birth representing other states as there were representing Indiana districts, and most of them ranked well among their colleagues—

Senator Wilson of Oregon; Lafe Pence of Colorado; Case Broderick of Iowa; Elijah Morse of Massachusetts; Senator John C. Spooner of Wisconsin; William M. Springer of Illinois; Joel P. Heatwole of Minnesota and others not so widely known. Is is not the purpose here to call attention in detail to soldiers such as Burnside, Canby, Lane, Admiral Brown, and dozens of others; nor to distinguished jurists from Blackford and Dewey to Mitchell and Elliott; nor yet to famous clergymen and educators, though in passing it may be mentioned that the pioneer of the American movement was not Lovejoy or Garrison, but Charles Osborne, an Indiana preacher.

Let us pass on to other lines that are commonly regarded as furnishing more conclusive tests of the development of civilization. It is generally agreed by students of the philosophy of history that one of the most conclusive of these is the financial system, and while this has been to a large extent controlled by national action, one of the most striking achievements of Indiana men—before a railroad had reached the state—before the Indians had been removed from its borders—was the inauguration of the phenomenally successful financial and banking system, which has been described in the preceding pages, of the State Bank of Indiana. Its success in a business way, and in furnishing the people a safe currency through a quarter of a century have been mentioned, as also its historical rank as the most successful state bank ever known in this country. Is it not a thing of note that this elaborate and successful plan was struck off with bold originality, and faithfully carried through to a satisfactory end by those pioneers? When the charter expired and the state decided to retire from the banking business, it was succeeded by the Bank of the State of Indiana, which filled its place in every respect except that the state owned no interest in it. It was, however, under state supervision, and while it lasted had a career as honorable and useful as its predecessor. It went through the great panic of 1857 unscathed, and maintained specie payments for a month after the general government had suspended them and made greenbacks the currency of the country. It was forced to wind up by the national tax imposed on state bank note issues. One of the men developed in the operation of this banking system was Hugh McCulloch, who is entitled to rank as the foremost financier this country has known since the war, with possibly the exception of Daniel Manning—a man who enjoyed the unique distinction of being called to the office of secretary of the treasury by three different presidents. Another who might be mentioned is J. F. D. Lanier, of the great banking firm of Winslow, Lanier & Co.

Another of the most commonly recognized tests of advance in civilization is skill in engineering. The records written in the ruins of Central America, as well as in the old world, the pyramids of Egypt, the old Roman roads, are all evidences of development more important than the preserved descriptions of the regal state of kings and the splendor of their pageants. This century has been one of mighty achievements in engineering, and of all the famous men who have made those achievements, can you think of one, American or foreigner, who stands higher than James Buchanan Eads? He was born at Lawrenceburg, Ind., May 23, 1820, and received the little schooling that he had in that town before he reached the age of fourteen. At ten years of age he was making models of saw mills and steamboats. At fifteen, while clerking in a dry goods store, he was spending his evenings in his employer's library studying mechanical and civil engineering. At eighteen, as purser on a steamboat, he was studying the details of steamboat construction. At twenty-two he was the inventor and builder of a diving-bell boat, and engaged in the business of raising sunken vessels and recovering their cargoes, which brought him both fame and wealth. In the course of this work he became better acquainted with the physical laws governing silt-bearing streams than any man living, and it is said that there was not a stretch of fifty miles in the Mississippi river below St. Louis where he had not

stood on the bottom under a diving bell. With the opening of the civil war, there came a need for war vessels on the rivers. Abraham Lincoln sent to Eads, and in a very short time gave him a contract for eight light-draft iron-clad vessels to be finished within 65 days. The timber for their hulls was uncut and the metal was in pigs and bars, but in 45 days the "St. Louis," the first river iron-clad, was launched, and the others speedily followed. They made possible the victories of Ft. Henry, Ft. Donaldson, Shiloh and Island No. 10. After these he built other war vessels and made the first application of steam power in handling heavy guns, by which he succeeded in loading and discharging 15-inch guns in forty-five seconds. After the war came the building of the great St. Louis bridge, in which he encountered and overcame obstacles never before met by engineers. With his wonderful caissons he laid the foundations on solid rock 90 feet below the bed of the river, and threw across the stream that great central span which is recognized as "the finest specimen of metal arch construction in the world." Seven years were passed in this work and then came the making of the jetties at the mouth of the Mississippi. The engineers of the United States army condemned his plans, but congress decided to let him attempt the work. His success in making the river open and maintain its channel is too well known to need comment. It made him famous throughout the world, secured him the highest honor from foreign countries, and caused him to be consulted as to important works everywhere. In 1887 he died in the Bahamas, leaving unexecuted his stupendous conception of a railway for carrying ships across the isthmus of Tehuantepec. Whether some other mind may carry out that project is uncertain, but we may have confidence that it could have been done by this Indiana man who so greatly reduced the list of conceded impossibilities.

You can hardly look for much development of high art in a new country. Wealth or leisure are essential to it. The artist must have a market for his work or must have the means of support while he works. All of our art development of any importance is of comparatively recent date. At our first Indiana exposition, in 1872, in the building that stood at the lower end of Morton place in Indianapolis, there was an art exhibit which was largely a novelty to Indiana people. One piece that attracted some attention was a painting bearing the inscription, "This picture was painted by a boy fourteen years old who never took a lesson." Think of the step from that to the exhibits that have been made in late years largely of Indiana subjects by our local artists. Of course, the comparison is hardly fair. We had artists before 1872. Many persons remember Jacob Cox and B. S. Hayes, who had studios here and did very creditable work. They had their pupils, too. Lotta Guffin and Miss Rudisell are perhaps the best known of those who studied under Mr. Cox. Hayes had two noteworthy pupils. One was Wm. M. Chase, now of New York and one of the foremost artists of the nation. He was born in Franklin county, near Brookville, and made his first paintings in Indianapolis. The other was John Love, a native of Ripley county, who, after studying abroad, opened the first art school in Indiana in conjunction with J. B. Gookins, also an Indianian. In this school most of our present artists began their work. Among them was T. C. Steele, a native of Montgomery county; Otto Stark, of Marion county; J. C. Adams (now in Muncie) of Johnson county; Wm. J. Forsyth, born near Cincinnati, but thoroughly identified with Indiana, and H. B. Williamson (now in Holland) who is also an Indiana man. Richard B. Gruelle is a native of Illinois. It is unnecessary to say much of our "Indianapolis group." Indiana knows them and shares in the pride over the attention which their excellent work has attracted. There is especial satisfaction in the attention they have given to Indiana scenery, and the demonstration they have made that we have here as fair subjects for art as are found in any land. Our most striking instance of phenomenal success in painting is that of our Terre Haute girl, Amalia Kussner,

whose wondrous art in medallion painting has made her successively the rage in Chicago, New York and London. What new triumphs await her can hardly be imagined.

There was another exhibit in that exposition of 1872 which has become of historic significance because it marked the turning point in the development of our Indiana sculptor—a collection of the well-known Rogers statuary. It was a novel sight to many Indiana people, and among others to one who had in him the nature of an artist. John H. Mahoney was born at North Vernon, Jennings county, Indiana, June 24th, 1854. His people were poor —his father a day laborer. He was serving an apprenticeship as a stone-cutter, working at the marble shop which stood on the northwest corner of Ohio and Meridian streets in Indianapolis—when the exposition was held. As he gazed on those miniature groups and caught their simple beauty, the thought came to him that he could do such work. He procured some artist's clay and without any instruction went to work. The figures he made attracted the warm praise of his employer, who at this time was called upon by the managers of the Franklin Life Insurance company to recommend some one to make a statute of Franklin for their building. He named young Mahoney, and the youth undertook the work. With no knowledge of the art of sculptor beyond the rules of the stone-cutter's work, by sheer force of native genius, he took a block of marble and chiseled out that figure which still stands in its niche fronting on Monument place. He took a few lessons in drawing and then made the statue of Gen. Sol. Meredith, which stands at Cambridge. In 1878 he went abroad, and for a year made desultory studies in the galleries and studios of Europe. He returned to enter into competition for art work in this country. He made the bronze statue of Martin McMichael in Fairmount park, Philadelphia; the bronze statue of Pierre Menard at Springfield, Ill.; the granite statue of Charles West in Eden park, Cincinnati; the collosal granite figures of "Liberty" and "Law" for the National

Pilgrims' Monument at Plymouth, Mass.; the statue of Henry Bergh for the public fountain at Milwaukee; and finally the statues of George Rogers Clark, William Henry Harrison and James Whitcomb for our Monument Place. It is gratifying that these, his latest works, stand in contrast with that first study effort of his genius, and it is safe to volunteer the prediction that they will be a source of great pride to the state hereafter. We may even venture the prediction that our George Rogers Clark will become as celebrated as "the Minute Man." We have another sculptor who is more widely known, George Gray Barnard. He was not born in Indiana, but was brought to Madison when a child by his parents. His father was a Presbyterian minister, who came to take a charge at that place, and still resides there. He early developed a fondness for natural history, first engaging in collecting geological specimens from the limestone cliffs, and then in mounting the skins of birds and animals until he became an expert taxidermist. The time for earning bread came and he obtained a position with a jeweler, where he soon became an expert engraver. His work attracted notice and he was offered the position of engraver in a large type foundry in Chicago. While there he entered the Art Institute. He began modeling in clay, and soon determined to have a broader art education. He made his way to Paris with very small means at his command. He struggled through four years of study and work. A stranger, a countryman, attracted by his talent, gave him timely assistance, and he wrought in seclusion until he presented the fruits of his labor at the Salon exhibit of 1894, including the portrait bust of an elderly lady modeled from memory; a portrait bust of a man in bronze; fragments of a Norwegian stove; a single sculptured figure, "Boy;" a group called "Brotherly Love," and the colossal group entitled "I Feel Two Natures Struggling Within Me." The entire group was acclaimed by the jury, and the young sculptor was elected a member of the Societe Nationale des Beaux Arts. In the year following Mr. Barnard returned to this country, and the same group of works was exhibited in the Logerot in New York, and was visited by all the art people and by many others in the city. The "Brotherly Love" group is in place in Norway. The large group, the "Two Natures," was bought by the late Alfred Clark, and was presented by the Clark estate to the Metropolitan Museum of New York. The "Pan," which has been so widely discussed in the daily press, has been successfully cast in a single piece by the Henry Barnard Bronze company, and is to be placed in Central Park. Mr. Barnard has recently completed "The Maiden and Pedestal," a figure for a mausoleum in Iowa. His latest projected work, a small model of which he has made, is a group of fifteen figures, all of heroic size, and entitled "Primitive Man," the pediment taking the form of a vessel and typifying the movement of humanity through the centuries and towards its final goal in the future. One of the figures, "The Hewer," has been finished and cast in plaster. It is a thoroughly artistic and marvelously lifelike figure, embodying an originality of conception and exhibiting a masterly handling and fineness of treatment that few sculptors have reached. We have other sculptors also who are attracting attention. The people of Indiana may speak with pride of Miss Janet Scudder, formerly of Terre Haute, whose work is attracting attention in the east, and who made "The Nymph"—a figure that adorned the Indiana building at the World's Fair, and which the people of Terre Haute happily secured for their city library. Another sculptress who has been winning laurels for the state is Miss Frances M. Goodwin, of New Castle, who made the statue "Education," which attracted much favorable notice at the World's Fair, and also the bust of Schuyler Colfax, ordered for the National senate chamber.

When we come to literature we of Indiana may ride down the lists as Ivanhoe, and strike, with grinded lance-head, full on the shield of the foremost champion. Let us pass all the lesser lights. What is the most successful American work of fiction of this generation? What has reached the approval of the people as no American book has done since Uncle Tom's Cabin? You must name "Ben Hur." The test of popular favor puts it at the head, though in the opinion of many it does not surpass in literary merit its predecessor, "The Fair God." What splendid work was this. How superb in its originality. How magnificently our Wizard of the North swept down upon the dull mass of commonplace, mistaken for realism, which was submerging the land, and with a stroke of his wand opened in its place a clear flowing stream of pure romance, a stream that has cut its own channel, and that is destined to flow on for the improvement and the delectation of future generations. Is it not true that the work of Gen. Wallace, possessing an absolutely unique character, and having achieved almost immediate success, has also the merit— not always accompanying these characteristics —which will make it live among works of literary genius? And the author is as purely a product of Indiana as can be imagined. And then our poet Riley. Did he not spring from our soil as old Antæus from mother earth? Did not his life take color from our life? Did he not drink in the beauties of nature as nature exists here? Was he not nourished by the wild fruits that grew about his path? Did he not learn how to feel, to think, to love, until he took his pen in hand—and then—

> From his flying quill there dripped
> Such music on his manuscript,
> That he who listens to the words
> May shut his eyes and think the birds
> Are twittering on every hand
> A language he can understand.

When Joaquin Miller, another gifted child of Indiana, whose words sound melody, visited Indianapolis in 1897, he stated that he came here to see and consult with one who had reached out to the hearts of the people. Therein lies the greatness of Riley's work, and therein its assurance of eternal life.

We have now noted some of the cases of notable development of the higher types in which we all take pride, and justly so, but these alone are not a sufficient basis for state pride. What constitutes a state?

> Not high raised battlement or labored mound,
> Thick wall or moated gate;
> Not cities proud with spires and turrets crowned;
> Not bays and broad-armed ports,
> Where laughing at the storms rich navies ride;
> Not stained and spangled courts,
> Where low-browed baseness wafts perfume to pride.
> No;—men, high minded men,
> With powers as far above dull brutes endued
> In forest, brake or den,
> As hearts excel cold rocks and brambles rude;
> Men who their duties know,
> But know their rights, and knowing dare maintain,—
> These constitute a state.

When you go over the whole ground you are forced to the conclusion that in a republic the safety, the honor, the prosperity of the state, depend on the intelligence and integrity of the common people. You cannot escape it. And you may have confidence in the people of Indiana. You may concede their faults. One of their worst is their failure to recognize the merit of their fellow-men. Of the distinguished examples that have been mentioned, very few received any recognition from Indiana until they earned it abroad. And our people do occasionally push to the front some of the cheapest demagogues that ever walked on God's green earth. But they mean well. We have seen them tried in the fiery furnace of war, and the superb record that they made when came the call to arms to preserve the integrity of the Union can never be obliterated. We have seen them tried in peace, and no people made a grander record than they made in their magnificent support of the purification of the ballot by the Australian election law. We have seen their sturdy adherence to the right in their support of the reform of charitable and penal institutions under the board of state charities law. We may see it about us daily in their efforts for better government, better customs, better morals and better manners. Look at their devotion to the public schools and to educational advantages of all kinds.

That means that they are ambitious for their children and for themselves. They are tired of the reproach of "Hoosierism." What is the significance of all the educational work of adults in this state? It is an expression of the desire to move up to a higher plane. And you see the same desire for better things not only in education but also in the material concerns of better public buildings, better streets and roads, better sanitary provisions, better everything. Our people have ambition, and so long as they have ambition they will be on the upward track.

We have therefore a proper and just basis for state pride in the people of Indiana. We have the conditions for the development of high types. We may not be able to analyze them, but you can all see that they exist from their fruits. Did you ever consider the miracle of the cherry tree? You see its bud, its bloom and 'its fruition yearly, but there was never a man so wise that he could tell how that tree stretches its slender fingers down into the earth and extracts from the great storehouse of nature the alabaster for its bloom, the emerald for its leaf and the ruby for its fruit. But we know that the needed elements are at hand and that it can gather them up. And so we know that in our state and our social organization the human soul may reach out and draw in what is needed to make it strong and healthful. We stand on safe ground and we have assurance in the achievements of the past of a still more glorious future for Indiana.